# SURFING INTO DANGER

All Eden wants to do is roam the coast surfing, at one with the waves and her board, winning enough in competitions to finance her nomadic lifestyle. But first the mysterious Finn, and then a disastrous leak from a recycling plant, scupper her plans. With surfing out of the question, Eden investigates. As the crisis deepens, who can she trust — and will she and her friends make it out alive from Max Charon's sinister plastics plant?

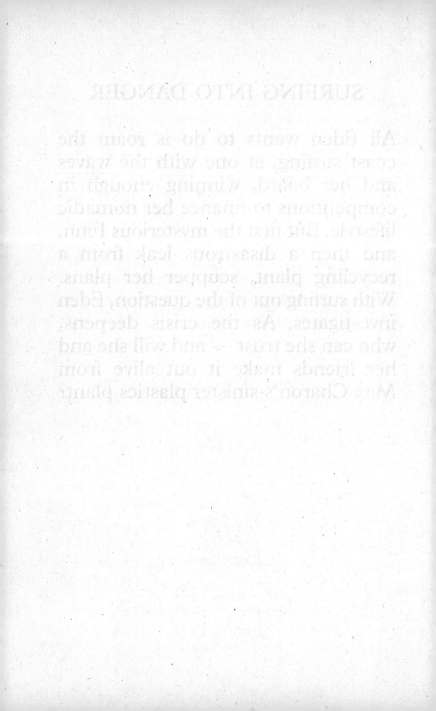

# KEN PRESTON

◆

# SURFING INTO DANGER

*Complete and Unabridged*

# LINFORD
*Leicester*

First published in Great Britain in 2019

First Linford Edition
published 2020

A catalogue record for this book is available
from the British Library.

ISBN 978–1–4448–4571–6

# 1

He had long, shaggy sun-bleached hair, a golden tan and the classic surfer's physique, all lean, rippling muscle. He was beautiful.

And right now, on this chilly morning in April, Eden Hawks wanted nothing more than to hit him and then storm off along the beach and back to the youth hostel.

'What did you think you were doing?' she yelled, resisting the urge to grab hold of him and shake him. Or maybe slap him in the face.

Surfer Dude, as she had already named him in her head, held up his hands. 'Whoa, hold on! Don't I get a thank you for, like, saving your life?'

'Saving my life?' Eden shouted and advanced a step closer.

Surfer Dude took a step back. From the look on his face, he'd suddenly realised how much trouble he was in.

Eden threw down the two halves of her broken surfboard and pushed strands of wet hair out of her face. She was thankful they were the only two people on the beach. That way there would be no witnesses when she murdered this idiot.

'I was perfectly in control out there,' she hissed. 'You were the one who crashed into me! If not for you I'd still be out on the waves!'

'Hey, let's calm down, all right?' Surfer Dude said. 'No need to go all Hulk Smash on me.'

Eden shoved him in the chest with both hands. He tottered and fell on his bottom on the sand.

'See this beach?' Eden threw her arms wide to indicate the long, deserted stretch of sand and sea either side of them. 'You could have chosen anywhere on it to surf. Anywhere. But you had to go and pick the exact same spot as me.'

The waves crashed onto the sand and curled around Eden's feet. Her wetsuit was keeping her warm, but she knew if she stayed out here much longer she would start to get a chill. April in Cornwall wasn't known for being warm and sunny, especially at seven in the morning.

Every day, Eden climbed out of bed early so that she could get down to the beach and surf and be on her own. Some days there might be another surfer or two around, but everyone knew the etiquette of early morning surfing. If you were out there at that time of day you wanted to be alone, just you and the waves. And so people kept their distance, gave you space.

Everyone knew that. Except Surfer Dude here.

Eden had spotted him on the beach when she was out on the water, waiting for that perfect wave. Sitting astride her surfboard, the ocean's swell gently lifting and dropping her, she'd watched him as he entered the sea with his board.

She had thought to herself, *Has he even seen me out here?*

Eden's perfect wave was heading her way. All of her attention, her instincts, had turned to the ocean, her board, the wave, as she had lain down on the surfboard and begun paddling.

Eden lived her life in the moment. Those fleeting moments when she was on her feet on her surfboard, the power of a wave carrying her fast and smooth, they were the precious ones. The moments she truly lived for and chased continually.

Unfortunately this morning's moment had been ruined by Surfer Dude crashing into her. The impact had thrown her off her board, and she'd rolled and tumbled beneath the water's surface. A strong undercurrent had caught her, pulling her deeper. Disoriented, Eden couldn't work out which way was up, and she had been dragged deeper underwater.

Until a hand shot out of the gloom, of the stirred up saltwater and sand, grabbing her and hauling her back to the surface and much needed, precious air.

Surfer Dude. Turned out he hadn't seen her from the beach after all.

'Can I stand up, please?' Surfer Dude said, still sitting where Eden had pushed him over.

She stared down at him, her hands on her hips.

'No, you can stay right there,' she said, and pointed at her broken board. 'What am I going to do now? The surf championships start the day after tomorrow! Do you think they'll let me compete without a board?'

'Wait one minute,' Surfer Dude said. 'Are you telling me it's my fault your board split in half?'

Eden threw her hands in the air.

'I don't see anybody else here, do you?'

'Aww, come on! I know we crashed into each other — '

'No!' Eden advanced on him, towering over him. '*You* crashed into *me* because you weren't paying attention.'

Surfer Dude held his hands up, palms out, in a defensive gesture.

5

'All right, all right! Please don't hit me!'

Eden stepped back. Was he making fun of her?

'All right, I'll admit, maybe it was partly my fault we collided — '

'*Partly?*' Eden yelled.

'Will you let me talk for a second? It's just, you know, have you thought that maybe your board already had a stress fracture in it, or something? That maybe it's not completely my fault?'

Eden said nothing. She knew she needed to calm down.

Surfer Dude ran his hands through his hair.

'Aww man, look, I'll buy you a new board, all right?'

'You'll buy me a new board?' Eden said. 'Seriously? You carry that kind of money around as spare change, do you?'

'Well, sort of,' he said.

Eden turned her back on him. She couldn't look at him any longer. Despite being utterly furious with him, Eden had to admit there was a part of her that found him very attractive. It was disconcerting. Eden wanted to, even needed to, stay angry with him. But she was starting to struggle a little with that.

So instead she looked at the waves rolling in. The conditions out there looked perfect for surfing. Not just getting in some practice for the upcoming championships, but for just being out there, one with the waves and her surfboard.

Surfing wasn't just a hobby for Eden, or a way of keeping fit. Surfing was a way of life. Since packing in her job as a manager in an obscure department in the NHS over five years ago, she had been on the move. She refused to settle down, always searching for the best surf, the best places to get out on the water and be alone.

When Eden was surfing, nothing else mattered. All the worries of the world disappeared, replaced by a sense of utter calm and well-being. Yes, constantly being on the move could be lonely, never settling down or planting roots. But Eden had had enough of responsibility and relationships. She'd been hurt one time too many.

This was all she needed now. Her surfboard and the sea.

But now her surfboard was split in half, and she didn't have the money to buy another. Which meant she couldn't participate in the championships and earn herself some much needed money if she did well in her class.

Surf Dude, obviously deciding it was safe to get back up, was clambering to his feet. Eden thought about turning around and giving him another shove.

Instead she took a deep breath and let it out slowly. But she kept her back to him.

'Hey, I was serious about buying you that new board,' he said.

'Great. I'm staying at the youth hostel in Covecliff, you can have it delivered there.'

'OK,' Surf Dude said.

Eden noticed the disappointment in his voice.

'What?' she said, turning around to face him.

Surf Dude shrugged. 'I thought, you know, maybe we could buy you a new board and then we could go for coffee or something.'

'Are you serious?' Eden yelled, getting right up in his face again. 'You smash my surfboard up, you almost drown me, and now you want to ask me out on a date?'

Surf Dude stepped back and held up his hands in surrender. 'OK, OK, chill, all right?'

'Do not tell me to chill!' Eden snapped, bunching her hands into fists.

'Hey, calm down, I mean, don't calm down, oh I don't know, whatever.' Surf Dude kept walking backwards, hands in the air. 'I'll get you a new board today, but who should I get it delivered to?'

'Eden Hawks.'

'Oh wow,' Surf Dude said. 'I've heard of you! You're, like, one of the rising stars in the surfing world, right?'

'Yeah, whatever.' Eden's anger suddenly drained from her, leaving her weary and sad.

'That's amazing,' Surf Dude said. 'My name's — '

'I don't care what your name is,' Eden said, and turned and walked away, leaving Surf Dude standing alone, his mouth hanging open.

She'd had enough. The day was ruined, and it hadn't even started yet.

Eden couldn't remember the last time she had been this angry with someone.

Or, she had to admit, this attracted.

# 2

Back at the hostel, despite the early hour, there was a party going on in the communal garden. Doug, a rangy Australian who never seemed to sleep, had lit a barbecue and was cooking bacon, sausages and large, flat mushrooms on the grill.

Eden's mouth began watering at the aroma of cooked sausages and bacon.

Ellie, a tall, stunningly beautiful Italian, hovered by Doug as he cooked breakfast. She kept gazing at him and smiling as though she was in love, but Doug didn't seem to notice. Ellie was new on the scene; she and Doug hadn't been together long.

'Hey, Eden!' Larry called, waving frantically as though they were separated by a huge chasm instead of the hostel's tiny garden. Larry was sitting at a picnic bench with his girlfriend Nina.

11

'Hi, Larry.' Eden wandered over to the table and flopped down on the bench opposite him. 'Hi, Nina.'

'How's the surf this morning?' Larry said.

'Cold.'

'Do you surf, like, every single morning?' Nina said. She was American, her voice a soft drawl like something out of the movies.

'Yep,' Eden said.

'You don't say much, do you?' Nina said.

'Nope,' Eden replied.

Nina laughed and snuggled in closer to Larry. They were both wearing thick jumpers and had their arms wrapped around each other. For a moment, Eden felt jealousy spike through her stomach. She envied them their closeness.

But she was happy for Larry. In the few years Eden had known him, Larry had been through a couple of relationships that ended bitterly. Nina had been with him for over four months now and this time it seemed Larry had found a keeper.

'Who wants a fried egg with their breakfast?' Doug said.

'No way!' Larry called out. 'You cannot fry an egg on a barbecue!'

'You think?' Doug grinned. 'Just watch me.'

He pulled out a sheet of tinfoil and ripped it into several squares. He folded the edges of the squares up so that each formed a cup, placed them on the grill and cracked an egg into each.

'You, my man, are amazing,' Larry said.

'I know,' Doug replied, smiling.

Eden smiled too. She felt comfortable here, with Larry and Doug. They travelled all over the world, chasing the perfect wave. Not together, not as a group, but they regularly turned up in the same location at the same time, chasing the same wave. And every single time it was like reuniting with family.

For the next few days Larry, Doug and Eden were all here for the International Surfing Championships. This was one of the biggest competitions in the surfing calendar, and not only did it offer valued prestige for the winning surfer but a hefty cash prize.

For Eden, like many other surfers, winning that pot of money meant she could keep her nomadic lifestyle going. Without it, she would struggle.

But now unless she found a new board and fast, she couldn't compete.

Eden was tempted to tell the others about her accident, about losing her board, but she decided against it. The last thing she wanted was to be the centre of attention.

'Have you met the new guy?' Doug said, flipping sausages over on the grill, the coals spitting as fat dripped onto them.

'What new guy?' Eden said.

'He arrived late last night, he was crashing about in the kitchen, making all sorts of noise.'

Eden shrugged. 'No.'

She didn't care about any new guy. Eden had to find a way of buying a new surfboard, and she had to do it today. Any new board she bought would need working in, and she would need to become familiar with it. That was a big hurdle this close to the championship.

'You didn't hear him?' Doug said.

'Eden could sleep through an earthquake,' Larry said, laughing. 'Remember that time we were staying in that hideous bunkhouse in Zanzibar and storm Etna swooped past us? I thought we were going to get picked up and thrown out to sea, the wind was that bad.'

Eden smiled at the memory. 'And I slept right through it and when I woke up in the morning, I was astonished to see all the storm damage.'

'Everyone else had been huddled together all night praying that we wouldn't die, while Eden snored away in the corner,' Larry gasped, laughing even harder.

'I do not snore!' Eden said, laughing too, her mood lightening for a moment.

'Have you guys known each other long?' Nina said.

'Maybe four or five years?' Eden said, looking at Larry.

'Something like that,' Larry said.

'Wasn't it here where we first met?'

Eden nodded. 'Yeah, I was still fairly new to the surfing scene, and you showed me how to wax my board properly.'

Larry looked at Nina. 'And there I was thinking what a newbie she was, and then later that day in the surfing competition she completely blew the rest of us away with her skills.'

'I was lucky,' Eden said.

'Luck has got nothing to do with it,' Doug said, and pointed a fork at Eden. 'This girl is a natural in the water.'

Ellie flicked her beautiful hair back and pouted.

'When are you going to teach me how to surf?'

'This morning, babe,' Doug said, smiling. 'But first, breakfast!'

Doug began piling sausages and bacon on plates. He lifted the tinfoil cups off the barbecue and slid the perfectly fried eggs onto the plates along with the mushrooms.

'I'll go get coffee,' Nina said, standing up and trotting inside to the youth hostel's kitchen.

'There are six plates,' Eden said. 'But there are only five of us. Who's the extra one for?'

'Finn,' Larry said.

'Who's Finn?'

'The new guy I was telling you about,' Larry replied. 'I'm surprised you haven't met him already, he got up early to catch the waves down at the bay. Didn't you see him?'

'Yeah, I saw him,' Eden muttered, her mood suddenly growing darker again.

'In fact, here he is,' Larry said. 'Hey, Finn, your breakfast is waiting!'

Eden glanced up as Finn approached. Despite the cool morning he was wearing baggy Hawaiian shorts and a T-shirt, with flip-flops on his feet. And he was looking right at Eden and grinning.

'Good morning!' he called out, lifting a hand in greeting. 'Wow, that breakfast looks great.'

'How was the surf?' Doug said as he placed thick slices of bread on the barbecue to toast.

'I don't know,' Finn said. 'It looked great, but I never got as far as riding a wave.'

'Yeah? Why not?' Larry asked.

'Because he got in my way, that's why,' Eden snapped, jabbing a finger at Finn.

'We had a little bump,' Finn said.

'A little bump? Is that what you call it?' Eden turned to face Larry, still pointing at Finn. 'This idiot snapped my board in half!'

Finn held up his hands as though he was surrendering. 'Aww, come on, man! How was I to know you were going to switchback like that? You came out of nowhere!'

Eden rounded on Finn once more. 'And how come you didn't tell me you were staying here? I gave you the address to send my new board to, you could have mentioned it then.'

Finn grimaced. 'You didn't really seem to be in a listening kind of mood. I mean, you'd already hit me once.'

'You *hit* him?' Larry said in astonishment.

18

'I did not hit him,' Eden snapped. 'I just gave him a shove and he fell over.'

Larry slapped his hand on the table and burst out laughing.

Eden stood up. 'Thanks for breakfast, Doug, but I've lost my appetite. I'll see you later.'

Before Eden had a chance to walk off, Larry had stopped laughing and grabbed her wrist.

'Hey, calm down, Eden,' he said softly. 'Don't do this. Sit down and eat your breakfast, all right?'

Eden considered wrenching her wrist free of Larry's grip and stalking off. But, she had to admit, she was hungry. And Larry had a way about him; he had a calming effect on Eden that nobody else had. He was a good friend.

She sighed and sat back down.

Doug slid a plate full of sausages, bacon, mushroom, egg and two thick slices of toast dripping with butter in front of her.

'Get that down you, you'll feel better,' he said kindly.

'I've got coffee!' Nina said, approaching with a tray laden down with mugs and the biggest cafetière of coffee that Eden had ever seen.

Everyone sat down at the large picnic table and began wolfing down their breakfast. Eden had to admit to herself that she started to feel better as soon as she began eating, and after the first couple of gulps of the strong, black coffee her mood brightened a little more.

As the plates began emptying the conversation picked up. There was talk of who was going where for the day, which were the best spots and the best times to catch a wave, and what the weather outlook was like for the upcoming competition.

The reason they were all here.

'I'm afraid it's not looking good,' Doug said, checking the weather report on his mobile. 'There's a massive storm out over the Atlantic and it's headed this way.'

'Oh man, you're kidding me!' Larry groaned.

'There's talk about moving the championship back a few days,' Doug replied.

'Is it really supposed to be that bad?' Eden said.

Doug looked up at Eden. 'Yeah, like batten down the hatches and hide in the basement kind of bad.'

Eden looked out at the perfect view. The sea disappeared into a hazy mist still clinging on despite the sun making an appearance from behind the cloud cover. Another hour and the horizon would be visible once more. It looked as if it was going to be a lovely day.

It was hard to believe there was a storm on the way.

Once the breakfast had been polished off, they all sat around talking and drinking coffee. Eden kept herself to herself. She felt better now, but she wasn't really in the mood for chattering. She noticed Larry glancing her way occasionally, checking she was all right. Eden gave a quick thumbs up to reassure him.

Eventually someone decided it was time to clear up and move on with the day. Larry and Nina volunteered to wash up, and Doug and Ellie began sorting out the barbecue equipment.

Which left Eden and Finn alone at the table.

They sat in an awkward silence for a few moments. Eden looked out to sea again, keeping her gaze averted from Finn. Anger and attraction twisted in her stomach like two fighting snakes.

Finally, Finn broke the silence.

'Look, I'm sorry about your board, all right? You're right, I could have chosen a better spot along the beach to go surfing.'

Eden turned to face him.

'Yeah, you could have,' she said.

And then she burst out laughing.

'What are you laughing at?'

'The look on your face, that's what,' Eden said. 'Were you expecting me to say, 'Oh no, that's OK, it was my fault really'?'

'Er . . .'

'You were, weren't you?'

'No,' Finn said, looking defensive.

'Seriously?' Eden said, raising an eyebrow.

'Well, urn, maybe, a little.'

'Yeah, well, you know what? There's no way I'm saying that because it wasn't my fault, it was yours!' Eden sat back and folded her arms. 'And you still owe me a new surfboard.'

'I suppose I do,' Finn said. 'How about we go into Perranbridge later today and I buy you one?'

Eden opened her mouth to speak, but nothing came out. Finn had floored her with his offer. Despite the fact this wasn't the first time he had offered to buy her a new board, this was still the last thing she had expected, and Eden had resigned herself to not competing in the championship after all. Surfboards weren't cheap, especially at the level she was surfing at.

But now it finally dawned on her that maybe he was serious after all.

'What's wrong?' Finn said. 'You need

a new board, right? You're competing in the championship, aren't you? Great, so am I. And I'd feel dreadful if you couldn't compete. So how about it? You could have a new board by this afternoon.'

'All right,' Eden said, nodding, still not entirely sure she could believe what she was hearing.

'Great,' Finn said. 'And maybe we could grab a coffee after.'

Eden hesitated. There was that offer of coffee again. A date. After her last relationship disaster five years ago, Eden had promised herself she was looking out for herself from now on and nobody else. Relationships were no longer a part of her life, and so far that had been working out just fine.

Finn noticed the hesitation. 'Or we can just look at boards and forget the coffee.'

'We'll see,' Eden said.

★   ★   ★

Finn drove them down into Perranbridge later that afternoon. He owned a colourful VW camper van, adapted inside to maximise sleeping space for himself and storage for his board and his kit.

'She's called Selena,' he said, as he wrestled with the steering wheel, navigating the hairpin twists and turns of the narrow country lanes.

'Who's called Selena?' Eden said. 'Your girlfriend?'

And why did the thought of Finn having a girlfriend send such a sharp pang of jealousy through Eden's stomach?

'No,' Finn said, laughing. 'My camper van.'

'Seriously? You gave your camper van a name?'

'Doesn't everybody?'

'I don't know,' Eden said. 'I never thought about it before. Anyway, how do you know she's a girl?'

'I just know, all right?' Finn said.

'OK, so you know somehow that your camper van is a girl,' Eden said.

'But why Selena?'

'Because I lost my heart to a Selena years ago, and I've never got over it.'

'So you split up with your girlfriend and then you name your camper van after her?' Eden said. 'That doesn't bode well for future relationships.'

'We were never a thing together,' Finn said.

'Seriously? You never even asked her out?'

'No.' Finn laughed again. 'She's a little out of my league.'

'Now you've got me intrigued. Why on earth would she be out of your league? Is she royalty or something?'

'No, nothing like that,' Finn said. 'She's Catwoman.'

'Catwoman?' Eden twisted in her seat to look full on at Finn. 'You mean, like, Catwoman from the *Batman* comics?'

'Uh-huh,' Finn replied, nodding.

'Have you ever thought that maybe she's out of your league because, you know, she doesn't actually exist?'

'Don't you say such a thing!' Finn

tapped his forehead. 'She's real in here.' And then he tapped his chest. 'She's real to me.'

Eden shook her head and laughed.

'You're crazy, did you know that?'

Finn grinned. 'Yeah, I get told that a lot.'

They drove into the tiny village of Perranbridge and Finn found a parking space. The day was heating up, and Finn no longer looked a little ridiculous in his Hawaiian shorts and T-shirt.

'This is crazy weather for April,' Eden remarked, glancing up at the clear blue sky.

'But great weather for surfing,' Finn replied. 'Come on, let's go choose you a new board.'

Surf It! had a reputation for being one of the best, if not the best, board making business in the world, not just in the UK. Run by Jim 'Corkscrew' Tiller, a past champion in surfing competitions all over the world, the shop was a family affair also involving his wife and two sons.

Eden had met Jim when she was looking for her first surfboard. They had instantly warmed to each other, forming a close friendship that sometimes seemed to border on a daughter and father relationship.

Jim was in his early seventies now, but he still looked as fit and strong as a man half his age.

'Hey, Eden,' he said, as she entered the shop. Jim had an easy-going smile, and he gave Eden a quick hug. 'It's been a while, how are you doing?'

'I'm good, thanks,' Eden said. 'How are you? How's the business?'

'A little on the slow side, but I can't complain,' Jim replied, and turned his attention on Finn. 'Who's your friend?'

Eden suddenly grew flustered, her cheeks warming slightly. The last thing she wanted was for anyone to assume that she and Finn were an item. Even though Jim hadn't mentioned that, she could see that look in his eyes and she knew how much he wanted her to meet someone and settle down a little.

'Finn, pleased to meet you,' Finn said, filling the sudden silence and shaking Jim's hand. 'We've come to look for a new board for Eden.'

Jim looked from Eden to Finn and back again. She could see the confusion in his eyes and she was afraid he was going to ask something personal. But then he turned and, all business, began leading them through the shop to the workshop.

'What happened to your other board?' he said over his shoulder as he walked.

'I had an accident,' Eden said. 'And it snapped in half.'

Jim paused. 'Were you all right?'

Eden smiled. 'Fine, it was just the board that broke, not me.'

'Glad to hear that,' Jim said, stepping through a doorway and into his workshop. 'Come on in, I think I have just the board for you.'

'Wow,' Finn said as he followed Eden. 'This place is amazing!'

Surfboards of all shapes and sizes

29

were stacked against the walls, or lay on benches waiting for work to be finished on them. A massive longboard hung suspended from the ceiling, polished to a high shine and glinting softly.

'Is that . . . ?' Finn said.

'Yes, that's the board I won the 1968 world surfing championship on,' Jim said, smiling. 'I never took her out on the water again after that day.'

'Must be worth a lot of money,' Finn said.

'Worth far more than any amount of money I could be offered,' Jim said, looking affectionately at the surfboard. 'I'll never sell her.'

Eden was off across the other side of the workshop, ignoring the two men. She had spotted her next surfboard, freshly waxed and ready to be put into the water.

Jim laughed. 'Well, I can see I don't have to introduce you.'

'Is this the board you wanted to show me?' Eden said.

'Absolutely,' Jim said, still chuckling.

'But I should have known you would find it all by yourself. The two of you are meant to be together.'

Eden ran a hand down the surfboard's length. In the water, on the crest of a wave, surfer and board needed to become one. The surfboard needed to become an extension of the person riding it. Running her hand over the surfboard, Eden already felt a connection forming.

Jim was right. This board was meant for Eden, and Eden was meant for this board.

'How much?' she said, turning to look at Jim.

Before he could answer, the squealing of tyres and the sound of metal crunching on metal interrupted him. The three of them ran through the workshop and back outside.

The two crashed cars were right outside the shop, on the harbour front. One was an old truck, its back filled with crates of lobsters and crabs. The other was a modern, sleek car, shiny and very new-looking.

The drivers were already in a heated argument.

'You should watch where you're going!' the younger of the two shouted. In a sharp looking suit and sporting an equally sharp haircut, he was obviously the driver of the modern car.

The truck driver was older, wearing the usual fisherman's outfit of dirty dungarees, checked shirt and oversized Wellington boots.

'Don't you tell me how to drive, sonny,' the old man shouted. 'I've been working these waters since before you were born. You've been here five minutes and look at the damage you've done.'

Eden leaned into Jim and whispered in his ear.

'What does he mean by that?'

'Don't you know who that is?' Jim murmured.

Eden shook her head, but before Jim had a chance to tell her, the argument escalated.

The fisherman had grabbed a wrench from the cab of his truck and took a swing at the car. It smashed into the driver's side headlight, shattering glass across the road.

'You'll pay for that!' the smartly dressed man snarled, pointing at the old fisherman. 'You'll pay for that with everything you've got. I only picked this car up today and look at it! It's ruined!'

An onlooker grabbed the old man's arm as he raised it to smash the wrench into the car again.

'Don't do it, Simeon,' the onlooker said.

'Let go of me!' the fisherman cried out, but he couldn't break free.

The younger man turned away, and it seemed to Eden that he paused for a second to look at her. Or maybe not quite at her, but something caught his attention.

A moment later, and with a last withering look around at the crowd, the smart man climbed back into his car and reversed away, spinning the car around when he found a wide enough space and speeding away out of sight.

Eden released a breath she hadn't been aware she was holding.

'Who was that guy?' she said.

'That was Max Charon's son,' Jim replied, grimly. 'And I'm afraid there's going to be trouble now. Big trouble.'

Eden turned to speak to Finn, but he had gone back into the shop.

*Strange*, Eden thought. *Why would he do that?*

# 3

Back at the youth hostel, Doug was unloading his car and carrying box after box of beers inside.

'What's going on?' Eden said, climbing out of Finn's camper.

'We're going to have a party!' Doug called back to her as he entered the youth hostel.

'Another one?' Eden called after him.

Doug came back outside.

'Sure, why not? Life's too short not to party. Hey, did you get yourself a new board?'

'I sure did,' Eden said, grinning.

Finn already had the back door of the van open. Eden leaned inside and slid the sleek new surfboard out.

'Whoa, dude!' Doug shouted, and looked at Finn. 'And you paid for that?'

Finn, looking a little sheepish, nodded.

'Are you like, a millionaire or something?' Doug said.

Finn laughed. 'I wish.'

'Jim said he made it specially for me,' Eden said, stroking the board like it was a dog or a cat. 'I can't wait to take it out and give it a try.'

Larry stepped out of the shadowed youth hostel interior, a huge grin splitting his face in two.

'Wow, would you look at that!'

'Isn't it great?' Eden said.

'Did you buy that?' Larry said to Finn.

'Yes I did, and no I'm not,' Finn said, holding up his hands.

Larry looked at Eden quizzically. 'Huh?'

'He's not a millionaire,' Eden said. 'Actually, Jim gave him a great deal on the board because, he said, it was for me.'

Larry shook his head. 'I don't know how Jim makes any money down there, he's always doing deals for customers. Most of the time I think he practically gives his stock away.'

'Did anyone hear about the accident down in town?' Doug said, pulling yet another box of beer from his car.

Eden never ceased to be amazed at how much Doug could fit in his car. Or how he managed to keep it on the road. Doug had adapted and repaired it so often that nobody was entirely sure what make and model his car had originally been. These days it was simply known as The Beast, and Doug showed no signs of ever parting with it.

'We were there when it happened,' Eden said. 'Jagger Charon drove his brand new Tesla into this old guy's fishing truck.'

Larry frowned. 'Ouch.'

'Then the old fisherman took a wrench to Jagger's car and smashed in one of the headlights.'

'Double ouch,' Larry said.

'Now bad boy Jagger's threatening to get his dad's lawyers to sue this poor old man.'

Larry's frown deepened. 'I haven't

got any ouches left, that's terrible. I mean, the old guy shouldn't have laid into Jagger's car, but he can't afford to be sued, it will cripple him. No one around here has that kind of money.'

Doug returned from the youth hostel empty-handed. 'Are you lot going to stand around talking all the time or are you going to help me?'

'How much beer have you got in there?' Finn said.

'Exactly the right amount for what we need,' Doug replied, grinning. 'Give me a hand with the rest and then we can go buy some food.'

'Food?' Eden said.

'I told you, we're having a party!'

★ ★ ★

Eden was itching to try out her new board, but she had to wait. A blustery wind picked up later that afternoon, driving the waves in random directions and making the surf useless for riding. As the afternoon stretched on, her mood darkened. The surfing competition, the only reason she was here, was happening the day after tomorrow and she needed to find out what her new board was like, discover all its quirks and characteristics.

And then there was that storm Doug had mentioned. If the competition was put back, that meant a couple of days trapped here in the youth hostel, the cost of her stay eating into her non-existent budget. She couldn't even use that time to practice with her new board because the weather would be too bad.

She sat cross-legged on her bed, watching the sea from her window. Another reason her mood had turned darker was Finn. Had she been too hard on him? Was it fair to have made him buy her a new board? Despite the knockdown on the price that Jim had given them, it had still been eye-wateringly expensive.

And yet, Finn hadn't even flinched when Jim told him the price. Despite what he said, was he actually rich? That would be a first. A surfer who actually had some spare cash was a rarity, never mind one with money in the bank.

And then there was that look that Jim had given her. The look that said, *hey, have you two got a thing going?* Jim was always hoping to pair her up with someone. Every time she saw him he would nag her about finding a boyfriend. Someone special.

Eden had no intention of letting that happen. She'd had her fair share of bad relationships over the years, and she wasn't about to start repeating those mistakes again.

So, why on earth couldn't she stop thinking about Finn? It was as though he had lit a fire inside her, and try as hard as she could, she couldn't put it out. But why?

Yes, obviously he hadn't been hit over the head with the ugly stick. He was downright, drop-dead gorgeous. So there was that. And despite having completely got off on the wrong foot earlier in the morning, they now seemed to be getting on well. And had Eden caught him looking at her once or twice when they were in Surf It! choosing her a new board?

She was sure she had. And every time he had looked away immediately.

Did that mean he liked her, too?

*Now hold it right there!* she said to herself. This was getting silly. Eden had only just met Finn, they'd hardly even started getting to know each other. And besides, wasn't part of her nomadic lifestyle down to Eden not wanting to settle down? Not wanting another relationship?

Eden threw herself down on her bed.

'Pull yourself together,' she whispered, angrily.

She stared at the wall and tried focusing on preparations she needed to make for the surfing championship. Everyone staying at the hostel was there for the competition, apart from Doug's new girlfriend, Ellie, and Larry's girlfriend Nina.

Doug was crazy, thinking about having a party tonight. They all needed to be focusing on getting some quality sleep and training. Even if there was a storm headed their way, they should still be focusing on the championships. The storm might change direction before it even hit the south coast, and then the surfing championship would go ahead as planned.

But Doug, he just lived to party. The maddening thing was, his lifestyle never seemed to affect his performance on the waves. Larry had once suggested to Eden that this was Doug's way of getting an edge on everybody else, that he tired everyone out by holding these parties while he stayed fresh.

Eden had just laughed, but sometimes she had to wonder.

Her thoughts roamed from the championships to Finn and back again. Why was it that she just couldn't get him out of her head?

Slowly, sleep began to wash over Eden and she dreamed about riding the waves, Finn riding his board alongside her.

★   ★   ★

'No way!'

'Sorry, man, I'm just the messenger.'

'No way!' Larry shouted again and slammed his fist against the table.

'What's wrong?' Eden said. She had just stepped into the kitchen when Larry had shouted, still groggy from her afternoon nap. But now she was waking up, and fast. She sensed movement behind her. Finn and Doug had heard the commotion and come to see what was up.

Martin, the youth hostel owner, turned to face Eden and said, 'The competition's been cancelled. I've just had a call from the organisers, they're asking me to pass the message on.'

'Cancelled? Why? I thought they were just pushing it back a couple of days once they knew where the storm was headed.'

'There's been some kind of chemical

spill!' Larry yelled and slammed his fist onto the table again. Eden had never seen him so angry before. 'The beach is going to be out of action for months.'

'Oh no!' Eden groaned.

'Ah, seriously?' Doug said as he pushed his way past Eden into the kitchen. 'Where's that come from?'

'Nobody knows yet,' Martin said. 'The slick's just getting bigger and bigger, and nobody's allowed in the sea. It looks pretty toxic from all accounts.'

'How long are they postponing the competition for?' Doug asked.

Martin shrugged. 'They're not postponing it, they're cancelling it altogether.'

'What?' Doug yelled. 'They can't do that!'

'Hey, like I said, I'm just the messenger boy. If it's as bad as it sounds though, the beaches and the sea around the shoreline will be out of action for a few months at least.'

Doug and Larry both groaned and Eden's heart sank. There went her last chance of grabbing some much-needed cash. A surfer didn't even have to win the top prize to get enough money, or a sponsorship deal, to be able to keep surfing and not have to get a 'proper' job. Eden never took sponsorship, she hated the idea of being tied down in that way. But she regularly earned prize money from surfing events — not a huge amount but enough to keep her surfing and travelling around the world. The Fistral Beach competition was a big one, and Eden had been hoping to come away with enough money to last her a few months.

Now it looked as if that wasn't going to happen, and for the first time in a long while Eden was staring at the possibility of running out of money. Which meant she would have to get a job, which meant settling down somewhere, growing roots. Before she knew it, she would be tied to a job, to a mortgage, to a life she didn't want.

Eden wasn't scared of working, and she never took handouts from anyone. But she couldn't get herself a job. After being totally self-sufficient for the last five years, returning to normality would be a huge shock to her system.

She turned around to ask Finn what he thought, but he had gone.

Again.

What was going on with Finn and his disappearing acts?

'Look, I'm sorry guys, but I've got to get back to the reception desk,' Martin said. 'If there's anything I can do to help, let me know.'

'Thanks, Martin,' Doug said.

'What are we going to do?' Larry said. 'I need that competition. I'm ready for it.'

'I know, I know, me too,' Eden said, placing a hand on Larry's shoulder.

'What are we going to do?' Larry said again.

'Well, we could have that party,' Doug said.

'Doug, can't you be serious for once?' Eden said.

Doug spread his arms out. 'I am serious! We've got the food and drink already, it would be a shame to see it go to waste. Besides, we can have a good time tonight and forget everything and then we'll find out more about what's happening tomorrow. Who knows, it might not be as bad as we think.'

Eden looked at Larry. 'It's not a bad idea. It will take our minds off the competition, maybe even help us relax.'

Larry visibly pulled himself together. 'You're right. Let's do that. I'm going to find Nina, tell her the news.'

Larry hurried out of the kitchen.

Doug looked at Eden. 'Did you notice anything strange about Finn?'

Eden scrunched her forehead up in thought.

'No. What do you mean, strange?'

'I mean, as soon as Larry mentioned the chemical spill, Finn turned and left. He just disappeared man, like a puff of smoke.'

Eden's insides seemed to shift and turn over.

'Really? I didn't notice.'

'Do you know anything about him?' Doug said.

'No, today's the first time I met him.'

Doug shook his head. 'I don't know, he seems a bit of a weird fish if you ask me.'

'What do you mean? He seems OK to me.'

'Yeah well, he just bought you a brand new surfboard, a Corkscrew special. That's another thing, where does he get that kind of money?'

Eden stuffed her hands into her pockets. The day had been warm, and she was still wearing a crop top, shorts and sandals, but all of a sudden she felt cold.

'Jim gave him a huge discount, you know what he's like,' she said.

'Yeah, I know,' Doug replied, gazing thoughtfully out of the window at the sea. 'And if it had just been you in the shop, Jim would have given you the board, I know he would have. But you weren't on your own, Finn was paying. Come on, Eden, that board wasn't cheap, was it?'

Eden shook her head. 'No.'

'And you haven't wondered how come Finn has that kind of money to throw around?'

Eden stared at Doug, jutting her jaw out.

'Yes, I wondered, and then I decided it was none of my business, just like it's none of yours.'

Doug sighed. 'I guess you're right. I'm sorry, Eden, I guess I'm about as uptight as Larry is over this cancellation. It's left us all up the proverbial creek without a paddle.'

'I'm going out for a walk,' Eden said, suddenly sick of this conversation.

She ran outside and headed down to the coastal path. The wind tugged at her hair and her clothes, but the sun was shining.

Eden drank in the sights and sounds of the sea crashing against the beach and the rocks, and the long grass on the dunes waving in the breeze. For the last few years, Eden had lived exclusively on the shorelines of the world. It had been so long since she had lived inland, she

49

had no idea what it could be like — what it had once been like. She just knew she never wanted to live there again.

But if she had no money, how could she continue her nomadic lifestyle? Eden refused to take handouts or charity of any kind. It was her decision to live the life she had chosen, independent and free, but that came with difficult choices and compromises. Perhaps she should find some steady work in a bar or something, if only for a couple of months to get herself back on her feet. She didn't have to grow roots.

But the thought of having to fit into a routine, of being pinned to one place, even if only for a short few months, filled her with dread.

As Eden rounded a bend on the coastal path, she saw a figure standing alone on a beach in one of the coves that dotted the coastline.

It was Finn. He was standing close to the water's edge, just out of reach of the waves lapping at the golden sand, and gazing out to sea.

For a moment, Eden considered walking on and ignoring him. After all, that had been the purpose of her walk, to spend some time alone with her thoughts. And Finn was probably feeling the same way, as he had come out here to this lonely spot of beach only accessible by a footpath.

But now that she had seen him, Eden had an overpowering urge to scramble down to the beach and join him. To stand by his side and gaze out to sea, wordlessly.

The breeze whipped her hair across her face as she hovered, indecisive and frustrated with herself. This wasn't like her at all, usually so single minded and independent.

Without consciously making a decision, Eden found that her feet had decided for her as she began scrambling down the steep footpath towards the beach. The path switched back on itself several times and there was even a dirty length of thick rope to hold on to at a particularly steep section.

Finally she reached the beach. Finn had not moved. Eden slipped off her sandals and picked them up and then walked barefoot across the sand.

'Hey,' she said as she drew near, not wanting to startle him.

Finn turned and his face, which seemed to have a cloud of darkness hovering over it suddenly brightened at the sight of Eden. The darkness was gone so swiftly, that Eden wasn't even sure it had been there at all, and that maybe she had just imagined it.

'Hey right back at you,' Finn said, grinning.

Eden stood by his side, looking out at the waves rolling towards them. 'I love the sea so much, the waves, their power. It's like nothing else on earth.'

'You're right, there's nothing like it, is there? It's beautiful.'

Eden scrunched her toes into the damp sand.

'Is the tide coming in or going out?'

'It's coming in,' Finn said. 'I have to

keep moving back so I don't get my feet wet.'

'Some surfer you are!' Eden said, laughing. 'Are you scared to go in the water?'

'Of course not, I just don't want to get these trainers wet, they cost me a lot of money.'

Eden glanced down at his feet.

'You could always take them off.'

Finn grinned at her. 'You want to go in the water, don't you?'

'Just for a paddle,' Eden replied, throwing her sandals back towards the dry part of the beach.

'All right then, let's do it,' Finn said, kicking off his trainers and throwing them over towards Eden's sandals.

They ran into the water together, laughing like children. When the rolling, swelling water got up to their knees, Eden smacked at the water's surface and splashed Finn.

'Hey!' he shouted. 'That's not fair!'

He scooped his hands into the seawater and threw it at Eden. She screamed as her hair and top were suddenly drenched.

'Right,' she said, strings of wet hair hanging over her face. 'This is war.'

They started splashing water at each other as the sea's powerful current pushed them from side to side. They both laughed and yelled, swiftly growing wetter and wetter.

Suddenly a particularly powerful current grabbed Eden's legs and pulled her over. She screamed as she fell into the water, her scream transforming into a gurgle as she disappeared beneath the surface. Finn's hand grabbed hers and he began pulling her back up. But Eden had other ideas. With a quick, powerful yank of her arm, she threw Finn off balance and dragged him into the water too.

Eden was back on her feet first, pushing strands of wet hair out of her eyes. Finn surfaced, spluttering and wiping at his face.

'I can't believe you did that!' he shouted, but he was laughing.

Eden started laughing too.

'Look at us both, we're drenched!'

Finn took her by the hand. 'Come on, let's get back on the beach, maybe we can dry off a little in the sunshine.'

Holding hands, they walked back out of the water and sat down on the dry, warm sand. Dark spots formed on the golden sand where water dripped onto it.

Finn was still chuckling. 'I only came out for a nice, quiet walk. I didn't expect to wind up half drowned.'

'You started it,' Eden said.

'Me? No way, you started splashing first.'

Eden laughed. 'That's not what I was talking about.'

'What do you mean?' Finn said. 'Oh, I see. You mean revenge for this morning when I accidentally knocked you off your board.'

'That's the one,' Eden said, laughing. 'I know you bought me a new board and all, but you still deserved a dunking.'

Finn chuckled. 'I suppose so. Is that it now? Have you forgiven me, or do I need to keep a lookout over my shoulder for any more acts of revenge?'

'No, we're all right now,' Eden said. 'We're even.'

'Thank goodness for that, I don't think I could have taken the stress of looking out for another Eden Hawks sneak attack.'

Eden wiped water off her face. 'The others are going to wonder what we've been up to.'

'Well, let them wonder,' Finn said. 'I don't much care what people think, these days.'

'What does that mean?' Eden said.

'Exactly what I said,' Finn replied, pulling his T-shirt off over his head and wringing it out. 'So many people try to box me in, expect me to settle down, get a job, buy a house, you know? I don't want any of those things.'

'I know exactly what you mean,' Eden said, trying hard not to stare at his ripped torso, at his chest and shoulders rippling with muscle and his perfectly formed six-pack.

'And then I get people complaining that I'm living off the state, that it's their tax money that is paying for my lifestyle, but that's not true, I pay my own way and I don't take money from anyone.'

'I'm the same,' Eden said. 'I don't own anything I can't carry with me. I don't even have a phone or a Facebook account.'

Finn laughed. 'Totally off the grid, right?'

'Right,' Eden said, and they high-fived each other.

They sat in silence for a while, gazing at the waves slowly approaching them. Eden's stomach was alive with apprehension and desire, with nerves and happiness. How long since she had last felt this way?

A long time. Eden wasn't used to these feelings, and they were taking her totally by surprise. Wasn't this one of the things she had been trying to avoid by becoming so independent? Living and travelling on her own, constantly moving from place to place, always in search of the next perfect wave, was a way of protecting herself from any more emotional hurt.

But right now, sitting here next to Finn, with butterflies fluttering around in her stomach, she wondered if maybe she was ready to build a relationship with somebody else after all. Despite their rocky start this morning, Eden knew she was growing increasingly attracted to Finn, and she was receiving the same vibes of him.

And then Doug's words intruded, pushing her thoughts to one side and unsettling her. *And you haven't wondered how come Finn has that kind of money to throw around?*

Here Finn was, talking about living off the grid, and yet he could afford to buy Eden that surfboard. Where exactly did his money come from? And why did he keep doing his disappearing acts?

Eden tried pushing the questions

away, but they kept nibbling at the edges of her thoughts. Her good mood quickly evaporated and all of a sudden she felt cold. She stood up.

'Let's head back,' she said, and walked off without waiting for Finn to respond.

# 4

Eden had woken early as usual. Despite the double blow of bad news yesterday, from the imminent threat of a storm to the chemical spill, Eden was still excited about trying her new surfboard. Covecliff was far enough from Fistral beach that its waters should be clear and unpolluted.

With her board tucked under one arm, Eden ran down the footpaths to her favourite cove. As she ran, she wondered if Finn might be there again. A part of her hoped so, because she hadn't seen him surfing yet and she wanted to know what kind of competition she was up against.

But another part of her hoped he would be there simply because she just wanted to see him again. Despite her misgivings yesterday as they had sat on the beach together, drying off after their dip in the sea, Eden knew she couldn't ignore the spark of attraction between them.

Maybe she just needed to ask him about the money, about how he could afford to spend that much on Eden's new board without it seeming like a problem. If they had a moment together alone today, she would talk to him. Finn would have a perfectly sensible, reasonable explanation and that would get rid of the niggling questions in her mind.

But first, she needed to surf.

As she rounded the final turn on the twisting path, Eden gasped at the sight before her. The sea had turned from its normal early morning steel grey into a shifting mosaic of bright, primary colours.

The chemical spill — it had to be. It was much larger than Eden had realised, and had obviously spread overnight, polluting more and more of the coastline. Eden stared at the sea, a wave of desolation washing over her.

Not just because she couldn't go out there and ride the surf, but because she grieved for the harm done to the sea and the life within it.

The natural world was precious and beautiful and needed protecting. And yet here was another example of the harm continually done by man.

Eden thought about simply turning around and heading back to the youth hostel, but something about the bright, primary colours shifting and stirring on the ocean's surface intrigued her. What kind of chemical produced colours like that? Eden followed the footpath down to the bay. She placed her new surfboard on the sand and jogged gently down to the shoreline.

As she drew closer, she realised this wasn't a chemical that was floating on the surface of the swelling, heaving ocean.

It was plastic.

The waves foamed and lapped at the sand by Eden's feet, depositing tiny pellets of brightly coloured plastic at her toes. Eden scooped up a handful. Where on earth had they come from? Why so many? And what, exactly, were they?

This was the worst case of plastic pollution Eden had ever come across.

As the waves continued crashing against the sand, Eden noticed a dead crab being pulled back and forth in the surf. This amount of plastic in the local water was going to devastate the marine life unless it was cleaned up pretty swiftly.

As for the surfing championships, there was no way that was going ahead.

Eden stood up, looking out across the revolting sight of the sea buried beneath so much plastic. Then she turned her back on it and walked away, without even having set foot in the ocean for the first time in years.

Back at the youth hostel the others were up and in a sombre mood.

Eden told them what she had seen, and Larry gave her the news that there was a public meeting scheduled in

Newhaven to discuss the problem. The plastic pollution had worsened overnight, spreading both north and south along the coastline. Many more beaches were closed.

The planned party hadn't gone ahead last night after all. Nobody had been able to rouse the enthusiasm and so the beers had stayed in the fridge and the meat had gone in the freezer. Doug had spent the evening online, messaging friends and contacts and reading the local news.

'There's a lot of anger,' he said, over breakfast.

Today's breakfast was a far simpler affair than yesterday's. Instead of a full English cooked on a barbecue in the garden, today's involved sitting in the kitchen, eating cereal and toast. Everyone was there, sitting around the huge dining table, but the mood was very different to yesterday.

'How bad is it?' Nina said, cuddled up to Larry but staring intently at Doug. 'Can we get gangs together and do a mass clean-up?'

'No, it's far too extensive for that,' Eden said, answering for Doug. 'After I'd been to my usual cove I walked up to Watergate Bay, but the water's polluted there too.'

'I took a look this morning,' Larry said. 'The waves are washing up a yellowy greenish sludge, along with dead fish and crabs. And it stinks.'

Eden nodded. 'It's a disaster.'

She looked at her toast, which she had hardly touched. Eden could feel a headache coming on. A nervous tension nibbled constantly at the edges of her mind. She needed to get out on the water, but she also knew it wasn't going to happen. Not here, at least. And with no money at her disposal, where else was she going to go?

She glanced over at Finn, but he had his head bowed. Almost as though he didn't want to be a part of the conversation this morning.

'Me and Ellie are going to the meeting later this morning. There's going to be some kind of announcement apparently,' Doug said. 'Hopefully we can find out who's to blame and then start fixing the situation.'

'We all know who's to blame,' Larry said, sharply. 'Charon Recycling, that's who.'

'Wouldn't surprise me,' Doug said. 'They've had accidents before.'

'Who are Charon Recycling?' Nina said.

'They're a huge recycling company, and their main plant is in Newhaven,' Larry said.

'But if they recycle, doesn't that mean that they are good?' Ellie said.

'You'd think so, wouldn't you?' Larry replied. 'And that was one of the arguments put forward against the locals who objected to them building a new recycling station there. That if we were going to help the planet, the recycling stations had to go somewhere, and the objections were a bad case of NIMBYism.'

'Nim what?' Ellie asked.

'NIMBY, Not In My Back Yard,' Doug replied.

'So the objections were overruled and the recycling plant was built and unfortunately there have been problems ever since,' Larry said.

'And the reason for those problems is Max Charon, the head of Charon Recycling,' Doug said. 'Max Charon has a reputation as a hard-headed and ruthless businessman, who is quite prepared to bend the law as far as he can to get what he wants. There was a lot of surprise at the news that he had got into the recycling business, and not everyone is convinced he is in it for the right reasons.'

Nina sat up a little straighter. 'Hold on, you said Charon Recycling? Are they any connection to Jagger Charon, that guy you told us about yesterday who crashed his car?'

Doug nodded. 'I'm afraid so — he's Max Charon's only son, and heir to his father's business and massive fortune.'

Eden glanced at Finn. He'd been

quiet since arriving at the table, and was sitting with his head bowed slightly. Eden wondered if she had upset him yesterday by suddenly walking off the way she had. It hadn't been intentional, she just felt so confused. So was he avoiding her now? Had she hurt him that much?

Eden knew she needed to talk to him, explain her misgivings and her uncertainty over the money he had spent on her. Try to clear the air. Eden was positive that once they had talked, they would both feel better.

She sensed something in him. It was as if they shared an emotional space; maybe even shared the same emotional wounds. And she detected a kindness in him that went deeper than the fact he had paid for her new surfboard.

But again, there was the problem. Eden had never met any surfer before yesterday who could have pulled out their wallet and put down that kind of money. With all his talk of living off-grid and being self-sufficient, how could he afford it?

Eden mentally kicked herself. She was just going round in circles here. The sooner they had a chance to talk, the better.

'Charon Recycling like to present themselves as eco-friendly and ambassadors for the planet, but in reality they are there to make money,' Larry said, picking up a slice of buttered toast and biting off a piece. 'A lot of money.'

Doug was scrolling through his smartphone.

'Hey, look at this. There's a rumour that Max Charon keeps a great white shark in captivity.'

'No way,' Nina said.

'Yes way,' Doug said. 'And it's right here, in Cornwall.'

'Doug, you really shouldn't believe everything your read on Google,' Larry said, laughing. 'Fake news, remember, fake news!'

'I suppose so. One thing's for sure though, there will be hell to pay from the locals at this meeting,' Doug said.

'This has affected us pretty badly with the cancellation of the surfing competition, but we can move on. For the local people, this is their livelihood. This plastic spill will destroy their fishing industry and their tourism. It will decimate the area.'

They all fell silent at that.

Eden thought about her dip in the sea yesterday with Finn. Now that spot would be polluted too, as the spill was being driven along the coast by the currents and the wind.

'What time's this meeting?' Larry said.

'Eleven o'clock,' Doug replied. 'You want to come along?'

'Absolutely, I'm coming along,' Larry said. 'Just try and stop me.'

'We should all go!' Nina said.

Finn suddenly stood up, scraping his chair backwards across the floor. 'I'm sorry, I'm feeling a little ill this morning, I'm not sure what's wrong. I'm going back to my room, I'll see you later.'

He walked off, clutching his stomach.

Everyone watched him. Even after the door had closed behind him, no one said a word.

Eden could feel the tension rising.

'What do you think is wrong with him?' Larry said, finally breaking the silence.

'He's in love, that's what's wrong,' Ellie announced, looking right at Eden as she spoke.

'What?' Doug said.

'It's obvious, he's in love and it's interfering with his system, with his nerves.'

Eden was painfully aware that her cheeks were beginning to warm up. She looked down at the table and hoped nobody would notice.

'Eden, are you blushing?' Nina said.

So much for nobody noticing.

'Ohhh, I see,' Doug said, as though he had just solved a perplexing maths problem. 'And it looks like Little Miss Sunshine may well be in love too.'

Eden stood up. 'You lot are just a bunch of little kids! Grow up!'

She stalked out of the kitchen, leaving

the others chuckling. She was not in love with anyone, and Finn most certainly was not in love with her. It was ridiculous. It was stupid. It was the most absurd idea she had ever heard. That was Ellie and her Italian nature, looking for love and passion where there was none.

And Eden had been acting like a teenage girl, thinking about how she and Finn shared an emotional space, about how she needed to settle down. She was being stupid.

Eden took the stairs two at a time, sat down on her bed and sighed. It was going to take a while for her to live this down.

★ ★ ★

They all met up later and drove into Newhaven for the public meeting. All except Finn, who had said he was feeling worse and couldn't make it. There were a few glances Eden's way, but thankfully no one teased her.

Traffic was heavy. It seemed everyone from the surrounding area was trying to get into town. The meeting was being held in the Town Hall, and when they arrived the hall was already packed with local people and other surfers. They managed to find space at the back to stand.

A long table had been set up on the stage and several official-looking men and women were sitting behind it, facing the audience. One was talking. Eden tried concentrating on what he was saying, but she couldn't make sense of it. Something about by-laws and zones and local regulations.

Once more her thoughts were drawn to Finn. She had only met him yesterday morning, yet it seemed she couldn't stop thinking about him. It was so infuriating! This wasn't the way she was used to living her life. Eden was used to being in control — not just of her surfboard and her body, but her emotions too. And now her emotions were scattered all over the place.

Larry nudged her, dragging her from

her thoughts and back into the moment. An old man in a very smart, expensive looking suit had stood up and held out his arms for quiet as a ripple of low murmurs ran through the audience.

'That's Max Charon,' Larry whispered. 'I told you Charon Recycling would be responsible.'

'I understand how upset you all are,' Charon said, his voice loud and clear through the packed hall.

'Upset?' someone shouted. 'You've just killed off our town forever, and you say we're upset?'

A loud murmur of agreement ran through the crowd. The grating sound of chairs scraping against the floor cut through the hall as people shifted angrily in their seats.

'Can we please have some quiet?' said the councillor who had been speaking earlier.

The audience calmed down.

'Yesterday afternoon,' Charon continued, 'there was a spill of plastic waste from our containers. The leak has now been sealed after a crew worked through the night to fix the problem.'

'It's too late!' a voice rang out.

'That's right, you've done the damage now!' someone else shouted.

Charon held up his hands again to shush the audience. 'I would just like to emphasise that the plastic pellets are the product of plastic waste sent to us for recycling, but the plastic is cleaned and completely sanitised before going for shredding into tiny pellets. There is no danger to health from them, they are not poisonous.'

'What a load of rubbish!' someone shouted. 'No-one can go in the sea with all that plastic floating out there!'

'That's right; you're killing this town!'

'Charon Recycling cannot take responsibility for this unfortunate event — '

The crowd's murmuring grew louder, turning into catcalls and boos.

The councillor banged his gavel several times.

'Please can we have quiet? There will be an opportunity for questions once

Mr Charon has finished speaking.'

'Charon Recycling cannot take responsibility for this unfortunate event,' Charon continued once there was quiet, 'as an investigation has found that the damage was done by a fishing boat trespassing in a designated no-go zone far too close to the recycling plant.'

The audience erupted, shouting and waving fists.

'You're saying this is *our* fault?' one voice rang out above the din.

The council official stood up and shouted over the general hubbub. 'Of course not, of course not, please calm down!'

Nobody took any notice. The hall filled with the sound of angry voices and chairs scraping across the wooden floor as people jumped to their feet.

'I think it's time we left,' Larry said, looking at the others. 'This is getting ugly.'

'Good idea,' Eden said. 'Let's get out of here before someone starts a fight.'

★ ★ ★

When they got back to the youth hostel, they found Finn packing up his camper van.

'Leaving so soon?' Doug said, the wind blowing through his long hair.

Finn threw his rucksack into the back of the camper. 'Yeah, I'm gonna move on.'

Eden's chest contracted painfully. Why was he leaving so suddenly? Was it her? Had she offended him that much when she abruptly left the cove yesterday after they had been fooling around in the water and then talking? Surely not.

And yet, here he was, leaving.

'How's your stomach?' Nina said. 'You look a lot better now.'

Finn grimaced. 'I'm feeling better, thanks. Still a bit of pain, but not as much.'

He hadn't looked at Eden once. It seemed to her he was doing his best to avoid eye contact.

'A pity you couldn't make it to the meeting in town,' Larry said. 'It was an interesting one.'

Finn looked like he was in pain again, but the others, especially Nina and the two men, were crowding him, hardly giving him any room to move. Only Ellie and Eden were standing back. What was going on?

Despite everyone hemming him in, Finn managed to slam the camper van's back door shut.

'Yeah, I'm sorry about that,' he said. 'I hope you get it sorted.'

He walked around to the driver's door.

Larry stopped him with a hand on his arm. 'Do you actually care about anyone but yourself? At times like this the surfing community comes together, but not you, apparently. You just look after yourself — is that it?'

Finn shook Larry's hand off his arm.

'Like I said, I'm sorry, but I have to go.'

'Let him leave, Larry,' Doug said.

'Yeah, we're better off without him,' Nina said.

Eden swallowed the tears building inside. Her friends were being mean to Finn, but at the same time she couldn't understand why he was leaving. Larry was right, the surfing community was full of men and women who came together in times of crisis. And yet here was Finn, leaving at the first sign of trouble and without any explanation at all.

This couldn't just be about Eden, and the way she had left him on the beach yesterday. There had to be more to it — something Finn wasn't telling them.

Finn climbed into the driver's seat and slammed the door shut. The engine started up with a puff of black smoke from the exhaust. Finally, Finn turned his head and looked at Eden, a lingering gaze which almost seemed to be pleading for help. But then he reversed and drove away.

'Good riddance,' Larry muttered, watching him leave.

Eden stalked off into the youth

hostel. She heard Ellie call her name, but ignored her. Eden had intended to go straight to her room, but instead she changed her mind at the last moment and headed into the communal kitchen. She filled the kettle with water and switched it on.

She realised her hands were shaking.

Once she had made herself a hot drink, she decided, she was going to take it up to her room, where she could be alone.

The others filed in slowly and quietly. Eden, unable to contain the anger building inside, rounded on them.

'Why were you so mean to him?' she yelled.

'What?' Larry said. 'We weren't — '

'Yes, you were,' Ellie said, interrupting Larry with her calm but authoritative voice. 'The three of you ganged up on him. He had no choice but to leave.'

Eden looked in astonishment at Ellie. She hadn't expected an ally.

'Aww, come on babe, he was leaving anyway,' Doug said.

'But he might not have, if you had given him a chance to explain,' Ellie replied.

Larry opened his mouth to protest, but Nina cut him off.

'Ellie's right,' she said. 'We ganged up on him. We were all keyed up and angry after the meeting in town, and we took our anger out on Finn, and we shouldn't have.'

Doug sat down and pulled out his mobile phone and began scrolling through it and tapping away. Larry was still standing with his mouth open. He snapped it shut and sat down.

'You're right.' He looked up at Eden. 'I'm sorry, we acted like a bunch of school bullies.'

Eden sat down at the table too, along with Ellie and Nina. She looked at her friends. How many times had they sat around this kitchen table, and many others like it around the world? These people would do anything for her, and she would do the same for them.

She sighed, the anger suddenly

draining from her body. 'It's fine. Nina's right, we were angry and upset. Has anyone got Finn's mobile number? Maybe we could call him and apologise.'

Doug leaned forward and held up his mobile.

'I haven't got his number, but I found something very interesting about Finn.'

Eden's chest tightened. What now?

'It seems Finn hasn't told us the whole truth,' Doug said. 'Anyone here know his surname?'

They all shook their heads, looking around at each other.

'Anyone want to hazard a guess?'

No-one spoke, but the sinking feeling in Eden's stomach told her she already knew the answer.

'Charon,' Doug said. 'His name is Finn Charon.'

Larry whistled. 'No wonder he wanted to make his escape so quickly.'

'No, that can't be right,' Eden said. 'You're making a mistake.'

Doug held out his smartphone for Eden to see.

There it was, a photograph of Finn alongside an article about the Charon family. Finn looked younger in the photograph and his hair was a lot shorter. Not only that, but he looked almost unrecognisable in a formal dinner jacket. Behind him she recognised Max Charon and Jagger.

Eden felt as if she could hardly breathe.

'Max Charon is his uncle,' Doug said.

'Finn and Jagger are cousins!' Nina exclaimed.

Doug was looking at his smartphone again.

'According to this article, Finn's dad and Uncle Max were partners in the company until Finn's dad died a couple of years back, leaving Finn a fortune in company shares.'

'That explains how he could afford to buy that surfboard for you,' Nina said to Eden.

Eden nodded. She felt incapable of speech, of thinking even. She felt numb.

'Does it saying anything else?' Larry asked.

Doug shook his head, his shaggy mane moving like it had a life of its own. 'Nope, I can't find anything else about Finn after this news article.'

Doug placed his mobile on the kitchen table and everyone sat in silence, contemplating the information they had just discovered.

'What are we going to do?' Larry said.

'About Finn?' Nina asked.

'No, about the plastic waste leak,' Larry said. 'Charon's blaming the spill on the damage caused by a local fishing boat, which means Charon Recycling won't have to pay a penny for the clean-up or in recompense for lost trade to the local businesses. It could kill off the local area completely.'

Eden stood up. 'There's nothing we can do. You're deluding yourselves if you think you can. Charon Recycling is a multinational corporation, with teams of lawyers and more money than you can imagine. They'll just walk all over us and hardly even notice.'

Eden walked over to the kitchen door. She paused and looked back at everyone.

'Finn had the right idea,' she said. 'He's gone and we should move on too.'

With that, she left.

# 5

Eden found Finn back in the cove — their cove as she had unconsciously started thinking of it. She hadn't known he would be there, she hadn't gone looking for him.

Feeling lost and abandoned, betrayed not just by Finn but by her friends, Eden had simply left the youth hostel with no idea of where she might go. The need to move, to get outside and walk down to the shoreline and be on her own, had driven her to her feet and out of the door.

With no destination in mind, Eden had found herself wandering along the coastal path again. She discovered Finn in their cove, standing on the beach with his back to her, gazing out to sea.

The scene was identical to yesterday, except for the sea crashing on the beach, waves topped with a noxious, multi-coloured, bubbling foam.

Eden stood on the path, watching Finn. Yesterday when she had found him here he had seemed contemplative, content even. Today he looked defeated, with his slouched posture and his hunched shoulders, his hands stuffed in his pockets.

Her heart ached for him, and yet she still felt troubled by his connection to Charon Recycling.

Finally she stirred herself and climbed down the path leading to the sandy beach. As she approached Finn he turned, and his face registered no surprise or pleasure at her presence.

'Hey,' she said softly, standing beside him.

'Hey yourself,' he said.

They stood in silence and gazed at the waves pounding the beach, pushing and pulling, the seawater hissing as it dragged at the granules of sand. The scene would have been beautiful but for the oily, fluorescent scum being deposited on the beach, the plastic pellets tangled up amongst fronds of seaweed.

'It's disgusting, isn't it?' Finn said, eventually.

'It's horrible,' Eden said.

Finn took a deep breath. 'I suppose you know by now?'

'Doug found you online.' Eden looked up at Finn, but he didn't meet her gaze, just kept staring out to sea. 'Why didn't you tell us?'

Finn laughed, but it was a sharp, unhappy sound. 'I can see how that would have worked. The Charon family business has to be the most hated name in Europe, and you think that would have gone all right when I told everyone who I really was?'

'You don't know what the reaction would have been,' Eden said.

'Oh, I think so,' Finn snapped. 'Look at how they treated me earlier, and they didn't even know who I was then.'

'They all feel terrible about that, they —'

'Don't lie to me!' Finn took a couple of steps away from Eden. 'I know what people are like, I've had to deal with it for years now. People are either repulsed by me because of their environmental beliefs or they want to be my friend because of my wealth. But no-one sees me, the real me.'

Eden stepped up close to Finn again. 'I think I do.'

Finn closed his eyes and bowed his head.

'Why didn't you leave?' Eden asked.

Finn sighed, and said, 'I don't know. It didn't seem right to leave, but I couldn't stay either. I drove around in circles for a while and then headed over here. I thought if maybe I just stood and took in the beauty of the sea for a bit I might feel better. And then I got down here and of course I'd forgotten that everything has been polluted now. And it's my fault.'

Pain sliced through Eden's heart at his words. She slipped her hand inside his.

'That's not true. You didn't do this.'

Finn opened his eyes at the touch of her hand.

'Maybe, but I haven't done anything to stop it, have I? All I've done is run away, and I couldn't even do that properly.'

'You couldn't run away because you knew you wanted to stay, that's why,' Eden said.

Finn slowly turned to look at her. He looked into her eyes. He had the deepest blue eyes Eden had ever seen, and right now she felt she could fall into them and lose herself forever.

'You're right,' he said. 'I need to stand up to my family. But that's not the only reason I couldn't leave.'

'Really?' Eden whispered. Her heart was galloping, her skin flushed.

Finn leaned towards her and touched his lips to hers. A tiny thrill of electricity coursed through her body. She pressed her lips against his, felt his fingers entwined in her hair and his other hand in the small of her back, pressing her close. She enveloped him in her arms, welcoming the embrace, the kiss.

Heat rose in the pit of her stomach

and spread through her body, setting her skin tingling. Every other thought left her mind, the five years of her nomadic existence, of her refusal to form a relationship with a man, of her dedication to surfing. For the first time in an age, Eden felt wanted. Needed.

Finally, reluctantly, they pulled apart.

'Wow, I wasn't expecting that,' Finn said.

Eden slapped him playfully on the arm. 'Excuse me! You were the one who kissed me.'

He grinned. 'I know. I still wasn't expecting it.'

They held each other in their embrace, foreheads touching.

'You should come back with me,' Eden said.

'I don't know,' Finn replied. 'I've kind of burned my bridges with your friends already — and that was before they knew who I am.'

'They're good people. Honestly, it will be fine.'

Finn said nothing.

'Besides, I'm not letting you get away now,' Eden said.

'No, I suppose not.'

'So, you'll come back?' Eden couldn't help the huge smile spreading across her face.

'Yes, I'll come back.' Finn looked out to sea, at the primary-coloured froth bubbling up to the shore. 'And I'm going to take action to get this mess sorted out. It's time I stood up to my family and told them that what they are doing is wrong.'

\* \* \*

As they approached the youth hostel, Finn tensed visibly. No matter how much Eden had reassured him that her friends would welcome him back, he couldn't quite accept that it would happen. They climbed out of Finn's camper van.

'Are you going to grab your things?' Eden said.

Finn shook his head. 'No, I'll wait

until I see if I'm welcome or not before I move back in.'

Eden took his hand and gave it a squeeze. 'Don't worry, I'll be with you the whole time.'

'That's the only reason I'm here!'

They walked across the gravel parking space. Eden could see them all, in the kitchen still, sitting around that big, homely table and talking. Larry noticed them first, his head bobbing up and then doing a double take as his brain registered what his eyes were seeing. He nudged Doug, who looked up too. His reaction was even more comical than Larry's, as his jaw dropped open.

Eden entered the kitchen first, closely followed by Finn. They stood holding hands, looking at the astonished group of faces staring back at them.

'Hey guys,' Finn said, a little sheepishly and raising his free hand.

Nobody said a word.

The silence stretched out unbearably.

'Look,' Finn said, gripping Eden's hand hard, 'I just wanted to tell you how sorry I am about — '

'No!' Larry stood up briskly. 'No, I'm not allowing you to apologise.'

Eden tensed, waiting for the arguments to start.

'It's me who should be apologising,' Larry said, approaching Finn with his hand held out. 'I treated you badly, and there's no excuse.'

Finn took his hand and the two men shook.

Doug was up from the table as well, and clapped Finn on the shoulder. 'Yeah, me too, man. I'm sorry.'

Finn smiled. His face was a picture of astonishment.

'Aww, come here, man.' Doug wrapped his long arms around Finn and hugged him.

'Group hug!' Ellie and Nina shouted as they jumped to their feet.

After they had all finished hugging, Nina made a huge pot of strong, black coffee and they sat down to talk things through.

Eden couldn't stop gazing at Finn.

Larry managed to catch her attention and gave her a smile and a brief nod. Eden didn't need Larry's approval of her choice of boyfriend, but she was pleased he was happy.

'I think I should explain myself a little,' Finn said.

'There's no need,' Doug replied.

'Only if you want to,' Nina said.

'I want to,' Finn said firmly. 'I've been on the road pretty much non-stop since my dad died. My mum died when I was little and I'm an only child, so there wasn't a lot to tie me to home. Uncle Max was keen for me to get into the business with him and Jagger, but that wasn't for me.'

'It's weird hearing you call Max Charon, Uncle Max,' Nina said.

'That's right. You almost make him sound cuddly and friendly,' Doug said.

Finn took hold of Eden's hand and gave her a quick smile before his face turned sombre.

'There's nothing cuddly about Uncle Max.' He paused, took a deep breath. 'I bet you'll have done your research, you know all about the shady deals, the chemical spills, the buying up of land which is then dug up, forests torn down, anything so that Uncle Max can expand his empire.'

'Which is why it's so difficult to understand how he got into recycling all of a sudden,' Larry said.

'I know, that's been bothering me, too,' Finn replied. 'He's closed down several operations all over the country in order to sink money into starting up this plastic recycling plant. He's not doing it for altruistic reasons, I can tell you that.'

Eden glanced at the others, at their faces, rapt with attention. So different to the situation only a couple of hours ago, when Finn was leaving.

'He's following the money,' Doug said.

'That's right,' Finn replied. 'I just don't like the thought of where that money might be coming from.'

'You said your Uncle Max wanted

you to join the family business after your dad died,' Nina said. 'Did you consider it at all?'

'Not for one second. Besides, he wasn't interested in me as such. The main reason I think he wanted me to join the family business was because Dad had willed me his shares in it. Uncle Max didn't want me selling them on.'

'And did you?' Larry said.

'Of course I did, I wanted nothing to do with him, or the Charon business. I wanted nothing to do with my family.' Finn took a deep breath. 'So I started travelling, had this idea I was going to see the world, meet new people, start a new life. But everywhere I went, every time I mentioned my name, it was as if a switch flipped inside people's heads. They either wanted to blame me for the world's environmental problems or become my friend so they could leech me for all I was worth.'

'And that's why you lied to us about your name?' Doug said.

Finn nodded. 'About a year ago I discovered surfing. This was what I wanted to do, but I knew I would have trouble with the surfing community if I continued using my own name, which has become even more identified with pollution since my father died. So I started using a new surname.'

Eden squeezed his hand. Finn had already told her this on the way back.

'Well, we don't blame you for your uncle's behaviour,' Nina said. 'It's like that old saying, you can choose your friends, but you can't choose your family, right?'

Finn smiled. 'Thank you for that, it means a lot that you were all prepared to let me explain.'

'Hey, is it true that Charon's got a shark in captivity?' Doug said.

Finn shrugged. 'I've no idea, but it wouldn't surprise me.'

'Forget about the shark,' Larry said. 'I told you. Fake news, man, fake news!'

Doug's phone pinged, and he picked it off the table and looked at the screen.

'Aww, no, I don't believe it!'

Everyone leaned forward.

'What's wrong?' Ellie said.

'Remember the old guy, Simeon, who was in a prang with Jagger yesterday? Charon Recycling have released a statement saying that it was him and his fishing boat that caused the damage and the plastic waste leak. They're saying that he's got to foot the bill for the clean-up.'

Finn stood up, his face turning dark with anger.

'It's a set-up. That's Jagger taking his revenge on the old man because he stood up to him.'

'Finn?' Eden said, looking up at him. 'What are you doing?'

'I'm going down there right now and talk to Uncle Max. This has to stop, now.'

Eden stood up. 'OK. I'm coming with you.'

'Me too,' Nina said, standing up.

'And me,' Larry said, standing beside Nina.

Doug and Ellie looked at each other and then stood up together. 'Us too!'

Finn laughed and shook his head. 'Look, I appreciate it, I really do, but I think it's best if I go on my own. If we all turn up looking like the Scooby Doo gang, Uncle Max will just ignore us.'

'I'm still coming with you,' Eden said.

Finn hesitated. 'All right, but just you.'

\* \* \*

They took Selina the camper van along the coast. As they twisted and turned around the narrow roads, the Charon Recycling building appeared and disappeared, but the noxious-looking cloud it belched from its chimneys was constantly visible in the sky.

Over the years as she visited this part of Cornwall, Eden had always been aware of the ugly building, with its inelegant angles and its silvery chimneys and pipes reflecting the sunlight, but she had always managed to ignore it too. All a person had to do was turn their back on the building and they would be greeted with the beauty of the Cornish beaches and landscape.

But now it seemed like a malignant canker on the headland, one that was spreading disease throughout the community. And in a way it was, with the plastic pellets polluting the sea and spreading along the coast.

As they drew close to the industrial complex, they had to pull up outside the metal gates, the first of what Finn promised were many security measures. Finn leaned out of the camper window and pressed a buzzer attached to a box with a speaker on a metal pole.

'Can I help you?' a tinny voice squawked.

'I'm here to see Max Charon,' Finn said.

'Do you have an appointment? I can't see that Mr Charon has any meetings booked today, and he doesn't see anyone without an appointment.'

'Tell him it's his nephew, Finn.'

Silence from the speaker.

Finn grinned. 'They'll be in a right flap now, wondering what they should do. Whatever they do, they'll probably wind up in trouble.'

The gate in front of them suddenly whirred into life and began swinging inward.

'I guess that's our invite to go in,' Eden said.

Finn drove the camper van through the gateway and along a dirt track to the front of the huge building. Now she was up close Eden was suddenly aware of how intimidating it was. The featureless, metallic walls rose high above them, their blankness interrupted only by the crazy criss-cross of narrow pipes shooting in different directions.

And then there was the constant hum, the low vibration in the air. If she had to spend much time here, Eden knew that hum would become extremely annoying.

From the parking area, Eden had a

view of Charon Recycling she had never seen before. There was the visitors' section of the building, with a set of double glass doors leading into a large reception area. Beside that was the more industrial part of the building, with a massive square opening in the blank wall. Forklift trucks were entering and exiting this opening in a regular fashion, and Eden could see the trucks going down a wide ramp inside the building.

This was a bigger venture than she had realised.

Finn parked, and they climbed out. The large, double glass doors slid open and a man in a sharp suit and sunglasses walked towards them.

'He looks like a secret agent out of *Men In Black*,' Eden said, and giggled nervously.

'Yeah, don't let the warm and friendly welcome lull you into a false sense of security,' Finn said.

The man approached, and said, 'Mr Charon, I'm here to take you to your uncle.' He looked at Eden. 'I wasn't aware we had another visitor. I'm afraid I will have to ask you to wait out here.'

'She's with me,' Finn said.

'Mr Charon doesn't like surprises.'

'Uncle Max won't like it if you offend his favourite nephew,' Finn said, and smiled.

There was nothing pleasant about the smile, Eden noticed, and it occurred to her that maybe Finn could be as ruthless and tough as his uncle.

The man thought for a moment, his expression unreadable through his dark sunglasses.

'Come with me,' he said, finally, and turned and walked smartly back to the entrance.

'Favourite nephew?' Eden whispered as they followed the man. 'Seriously?'

'All right, maybe I should have said 'only nephew',' Finn replied.

They entered a stark, utilitarian reception area, their footsteps echoing through the vast space. That hum was still there, a soft vibration running through the walls, floor, everything.

They stepped into a lift and the doors slid shut with a soft sigh. The man swiped a pass at a blank plate in the lift's control panel, and the doors slid shut. The three of them stood in silence as the lift made its way down, much to Eden's surprise. There were only two buttons on the control panel, and neither of them indicated that the lift was able to descend to a lower floor.

The doors opened onto a carpeted hall that could have been in an upmarket hotel. Stepping out of the lift, Eden realised the hum had stopped — or maybe just wasn't detectable down here.

Glancing at Finn as the man led them down the short, wide corridor, Eden wondered how far underground they were. Glancing behind her she noticed a set of stairs leading up, beside the elevator. A fire escape, she guessed.

The man, still wearing his sunglasses, stopped outside a large pair of wooden panelled doors. He knocked briskly, then swung both doors open and stepped back to let Eden and Finn walk through.

Eden gasped. Not at the huge room with the large desk and the comfortable chairs and sofas scattered throughout the carpeted space, nor at the massive, boardroom-style table with empty chairs positioned all around it, or the vast, abstract oil paintings hanging from the walls.

No — she gasped at the view through the massive picture window behind the desk.

They were underwater, but the view had been lit up with powerful arc lamps illuminating the sea bed and its variety of life. Eden saw crabs scuttling across the rocky ground, and fish of all shapes and sizes swimming in lazy circles.

Max Charon might not have a great white shark in captivity, but he had plenty of other marine life.

Before she had time to fully take in what she was seeing, she was interrupted by an old man dressed in a smart and expensive looking suit approaching them with his hands held out.

'Finn! How wonderful to see you!'

'Uncle Max,' Finn replied, his tone rather more reserved.

Max Charon lowered his arms once he realised he wasn't going to get a hug from his nephew and the two men shook hands instead. Charon then turned his gaze upon Eden.

'And who is this beautiful young lady you have brought with you?' he said, looking Eden up and down. Eden felt as though she had a hundred spiders crawling over her flesh.

'This is Eden, a good friend of mine,' Finn said.

Charon nodded appreciatively and then turned his attention back to Finn.

'Let me get you both a drink,' he said. 'Tea? Coffee? Or something a little stronger?'

'No, nothing, thank you,' Eden and Finn both said, stumbling a little over their words.

'Nonsense!' Charon strode over to his desk and punched a button. 'Mary, tea please.' Charon turned back to his guests. 'Sit down, sit down,' he said, indicating the leather sofas.

Eden and Finn sat down next to each other on one sofa, and Charon sat opposite at his desk. On the surface of the desk lay a few scattered sheets of coloured paper of various sizes, and a pair of black-handled scissors.

'Finn, please tell me that you have changed your mind and you are returning to the family business,' Charon said, clasping his hands together. 'Your father would be so proud.'

Finn shook his head.

'I'm sorry, Uncle Max, that's not why I'm here.'

'That's a shame,' Charon said, 'because we need you back.'

Eden found herself drawn again to the beautiful underwater scene. There was something wrong with it. It looked too real — hyper-real. As though the view was of a sub-tropical climate or a barrier reef. Not the typical British sea.

And then there was the fact of the plastic pellets spill. Eden had already seen dead fish washing up on the shore and the toxic sludge in the water. How could this one spot just outside the window be immune to the damage being done elsewhere along the shoreline?

'I see you are admiring the view,' Charon said. 'Quite something, isn't it?'

'Yes, it is,' Eden replied. 'But it doesn't seem real. I mean, it can't be real — we don't have that kind of marine life here in Britain.'

'Quite correct,' Charon said. 'What you are looking at is a huge aquarium, one of the largest in the world, housing all manner of exotic marine species, built on the ocean floor and enclosed in ultra-strong polymer plastic casings.'

'I see you're spending the Charon family money wisely,' Finn remarked.

'I'm protecting endangered species, that's what I am doing, Finn,' Charon snapped, turning on his nephew.

'Despite my reputation, I am a conservationist at heart.'

'Is that why the locals are now dealing with a massive spill from your factory that is decimating the local marine life and will destroy the economy?' Finn said.

'The unfortunate incident with the shredded plastic waiting for recycling wasn't the fault of Charon Recycling,' the old man said quietly but powerfully. 'That was caused by a local fisherman trespassing in a private area, and damaging a cable with his anchor.'

'And now you're going to lay the cost of the clean-up on him, an old man who scratches out a living at sea and hasn't got two pennies to rub together?' Eden said.

Charon sat back, a look of surprise on his lined face. 'Why no, of course not! What do you think I am, some kind of monster?'

A movement on the other side of the large window caught Eden's eye, and she turned to look and gasped.

'You have a great white shark?' she whispered.

The great white was gliding slowly past the window, its powerful tail fin flicking from side to side and propelling it through the water. Eden just caught a glimpse of its mouth, at rows of serrated teeth, before it turned and swam away.

The rumour was true after all.

'Ah yes, the prize of my collection,' Charon said, rising from his seat and walking over to the picture window. He placed a hand against the glass as the shark swam past once more.

Eden shivered. She wasn't sure which one was the true predator, the shark or the old man.

Charon spoke, but remained facing the glass, watching the shark as it swam away. 'I named him. Bruce, after my lawyer. Sharks, lawyers, they're the same thing really, aren't they?'

Finn stood up. 'Uncle Max,' he said.

The old man turned around.

'Were you serious? You're not going

to prosecute the fisherman, or make him liable for the damage?'

'Yes, I was totally serious,' Charon said. 'I'm not in the business of ruining people's lives. In fact, I have some of my people visiting him now, and putting his mind at ease. Despite the fact that he was plainly trespassing, Charon Recycling shall not be holding him liable for the damage he caused, or for the costs of the clean-up necessitated by the spill, again through no fault of ours but the damage caused by his trespassing on our property. And the clean-up starts tomorrow, by the way! I owe a debt of thanks to the locals for allowing me to site Charon Recycling here, and paying to put right this unfortunate situation is the least I can do.'

Eden and Finn looked at each other. This was the last response either of them had expected.

'Finn! What a pleasant surprise!'

Jagger Charon stood in the open doorway. Hair gelled into spikes, shirt collar casually undone and tie pulled loose, he looked like he had just finished a cover shoot for a magazine.

'Hello, Jagger,' Finn said, his voice cool and reserved.

Eden suppressed the shiver that ran through her at the sight of Finn's cousin. It seemed to her that yet another predator had entered the room.

It was a pity only one of them was behind glass.

# 6

Jagger pumped Finn's hand as if shaking someone's hand in greeting was an Olympic sport and he was determined to win.

Then he turned and looked Eden up and down, much as his father had. It seemed he wasn't all that impressed, as he turned his attention back to Finn without a word of greeting to Eden.

'Have you returned to your senses?' Jagger said. 'Have you finished acting like a beach bum and come back to the real world?'

Finn shook his head and laughed bitterly.

'No, I don't think so. How about you, Jagger? I see you're still driving flash cars too fast and ruining lives.'

Jagger grinned. 'I thought I saw you on the quay the other day, lurking in the background. That old guy should have been watching where he was going. Did you see his truck? It's a deathtrap.'

'It's also his livelihood,' Eden snapped. 'And you almost took it away from him.'

'Let's all calm down,' Max Charon said. 'Jagger, please show some respect to our guest, Eden.'

Jagger smiled at Eden, revealing perfect white teeth. Eden couldn't help but be reminded of the shark, swimming in circles in Charon's tank.

'Yes, I apologise,' Jagger said. 'I am being very rude, aren't I?'

'In fact, Finn, why don't you and your lady friend stay for dinner?' Charon said.

Finn looked at Eden and she stared back, willing him to say no.

'Thank you for the invite,' Finn said to Charon, 'but we really need to get back.'

'A pity. Maybe another time. Before you go, I have something for you, young lady.'

Charon pulled open a drawer in his desk and took something out. It was a shade of pastel blue, like the sheets of paper on his desk. Charon picked up the scissors and made a couple of snips here and there. He put the scissors in the drawer, made a couple of final folds in the paper and then walked around the desk and presented his creation to Eden.

'For you,' he said. 'A reminder of your friends in the ocean.'

Eden took the tiny shark made of folded paper.

'Wow,' she said. 'This is amazing. You made it?'

Charon smiled. 'A little hobby of mine, origami.'

Eden turned the fragile paper shark around in her hand. It was perfect.

'Finn, please don't be a stranger any more,' Charon said. 'You and Eden are welcome any time.'

Finn nodded at his uncle and they shook hands.

'I'll show you out,' Jagger said, flashing his shark's smile at Eden again.

Charon shook hands with Eden.

'Don't believe everything you hear about me. Really, I'm one of the good guys.'

Jagger led them out of the huge board room and they stepped into the lift, where Jagger swiped his pass across the blank plate beneath the buttons for the ground and first floor. The doors slid shut, and they began rising.

'It's beyond me, but the old man's got a soft spot for you, for some reason,' Jagger said. 'But not me. I think you're trouble, Finn. And you should stay away, before things turn nasty.'

Eden's heart turned cold at Jagger's words.

'Is that a threat?' Finn said.

'Nah, think of it as a piece of advice,' Jagger replied. 'A nice, friendly piece of advice to my favourite cousin.'

The lift slowed to a halt, and the doors slid open. The man in the suit and sunglasses was waiting for them. The hum, barely discernible, vibrating through the walls and floor had returned.

'Go on, leave,' Jagger whispered to Finn. 'Take your girlfriend with you and don't come back. You're an embarrassment.'

Finn held Jagger's gaze for a long moment and then took Eden's hand. They stepped out of the elevator. Finn didn't look back as they walked through the complex and reception until they were back outside.

'What a horrible person,' Eden said.

'Which one?' Finn said, as they walked back to his campervan.

'Jagger,' Eden replied. 'But your uncle Max, I couldn't work him out. At first I didn't like him, but now he's told us he's not going to prosecute Simeon, I'm not so sure.' She looked at the paper shark in her hand. 'And this is beautiful.'

'Origami has always been a passion of his. Ever since I was a youngster I can remember him giving me paper animals and aeroplanes,' Finn said. 'But don't be taken in by all that flannel. He's up to something, I'm sure.'

'Oh.' Eden's heart sank. She had hoped this might all be over — that Simeon was going to be free from the threat of prosecution and that the shoreline would soon be cleaned up — but it didn't sound that way.

They climbed back into the camper van and Finn gunned the engine into noisy life, black smoke belching from the exhaust behind them. The gate was already open for them and they were able to drive straight through without stopping.

Eden held the origami shark up, and said, 'Hey Bruce, what do you think we should do?'

Bruce didn't reply.

As they drove along the coastal path they saw teams of people along the beaches collecting rubbish and dead fish, filling large bin bags.

'This is what community is all about,' Finn said. 'People volunteering to clean up the mess made by somebody else. And I bet you anything, as well as locals doing the hard work of cleaning up, there will be holidaymakers too.'

'Everyone's becoming more aware of the damage we are doing to our planet,' Eden said. 'The message is getting through that we need to be more responsible.'

'But then you've got idiots like my uncle and cousin, who are still intent on polluting the ocean, even though they claim to be environmentalists at heart.'

'What do we do now?' Eden said.

'I don't know,' Finn muttered.

'How about we get down on one of those beaches and start helping with the clean-up?'

Finn grinned. 'That's a good idea.'

★  ★  ★

The rest of the group at the youth hostel had already had the same idea. Doug had been out and bought some industrial strength rubber gloves to protect their hands from any nasty chemicals there might be in the sea along with the plastic pellets, and several rolls of bin bags to collect rubbish in.

Eden and Finn quickly filled everyone in on their meeting with the Charons.

Nina said, 'Maybe we should go and visit Simeon, find out what Max Charon's men said to him.'

'That's a good idea,' said Larry. 'The thought of Max Charon's men visiting me sets my flesh crawling, so I hate to think how it might have gone when they paid that poor old man a visit.'

Together they made a plan to do a beach clean first, then Eden and Finn could visit Simeon while the others returned to the hostel and planned a barbecue and party. The last bit was Doug's idea.

They headed down to Watergate Bay, and Eden was shocked at all the debris being washed up on the beach. Along with the plastic pellets there were plastic bottles and containers, colourful shards of plastic which Eden could not identify, wrappers and clingmfilm. There was just so much.

Eden's next emotion, after the shock, was despair. How on earth could they hope to clean this mess up? However much they managed to collect today, there would probably be an equal amount deposited on the beach again by tomorrow morning. And was it still escaping into the sea from the Charon Recycling containers? How much of this stuff did they have?

But then Eden looked at the small crowd of men, women and children already on the beach picking up litter, and she knew there was hope. She knew that no matter how often the sea threw humanity's rubbish and pollution back at them, these people would be there to collect it and dispose of it properly.

They spent a couple of hours walking up and down the beach, collecting rubbish. Once the beach was looking cleaner and healthier, they split up, Eden and Finn heading into town while the others made their way back to the hostel.

Eden noticed the wind had started picking up, blowing in powerful gusts. Was the storm on its way? Something else to worry about. Not only was the storm threatening Eden's perilous financial situation by causing the cancellation of the surfing championships, but it would disperse the plastic pollution further.

They visited Jim's surf shop first, to find out Simeon's address. Jim knew pretty much everything about everyone in the local area.

Jim was in the workshop, shaving long slivers of foam off a new board he was making.

'Hey, how's the surfboard?' Jim asked Eden, his lined face splitting into a huge smile.

Eden scowled. 'I haven't had a chance to go out on the water yet, what with this pollution.'

'That's a shame,' Jim said. 'You need to get some practice in before the competition.'

'But that's been cancelled,' Eden said.

'Not any more,' Jim replied, running his hands along a freshly smoothed new board. 'The organisers have moved the competition to Partington Rocks. It's all happening on Thursday.'

'Are you sure?' Finn said. 'We haven't heard anything.'

'There's an announcement going out later this afternoon. By that point they're hoping that the storm will have passed over, and the conditions should be ideal.' Jim looked at Eden. 'If you want to be in with a chance of winning that cash prize, you'd better get back out on the water, and soon.'

Eden dropped her head into her hands.

'I don't believe it. A new location and a new board? And the competition's the day after tomorrow. How will I be ready in time?'

'Just keep your cool, and you'll be fine.' Jim chuckled. 'Anyway, what can I do for you guys?'

'We wondered if you know where Simeon lives,' Eden said.

Jim nodded, thoughtfully. 'Yes, I do. Are you planning on paying him a visit? He doesn't much like visitors, he's a very private man.'

'That's a shame,' Finn said, 'because

he's already had one visit from a team of Max Charon's lawyers.'

Jim looked quizzically from Finn to Eden.

'Tell me more.'

They quickly filled him in on their visit to Charon Labs and what Max Charon had told them.

Jim shook his head slowly. 'This isn't good. Poor Simeon is a vulnerable old man. He never was much of a sociable kind of person, but since his wife died a few years back, he's practically turned into a hermit.'

'Oh no, that's awful,' Eden said. 'I wonder how he felt, confronted by Charon's lawyers? It must have been terrifying for him.'

'And you don't believe what Max Charon told you, that they weren't going to prosecute him?' Jim asked.

'No, I don't believe him one bit,' Finn muttered darkly. 'My uncle Max will take any opportunity he can to duck responsibility for the pollution they've caused by laying the blame on Simeon.'

'This could finish him off,' Jim said. 'Look, why don't I come with you? Simeon knows me, and he trusts me. He'll never let you in his house if you just rock up on his doorstep, but with me there to vouch for you . . . well, he might let you in.'

★  ★  ★

The fisherman lived in one of the oldest parts of town. Many of the houses had been renovated in the last ten years or so and bought up for holiday lets, but there were a few, like Simeon's, that hadn't. His small, terraced house stood out from the rest by its appearance. The black stone walls were covered in creeping ivy, and the windows were dark and filthy. Net curtains that hadn't been washed in years hung in the windows. A black cat on the sill and gazed through the dirt smeared glass at the newcomers.

'I have to warn you,' Jim said, just before he knocked on the door, 'the inside is worse. Simeon doesn't look after himself particularly well. Over the years a few of us have tried to organise getting someone in regularly to clean and cook for him, but he's a very proud man and won't have any of it.'

Jim rapped on the door and they waited.

And waited.

Eden thought she saw the net curtain twitching.

'I think he's in there,' she said.

'I'm sure he is,' Jim replied. 'But that doesn't mean he'll open the door and welcome us in.'

'Should we knock again?' Finn said.

Jim shook his head. 'No, that will just scare him off. Let's wait a little longer, he might open the door for us.'

They waited, Eden feeling increasingly twitchy and impatient. She had been feeling this way since Jim had told her the surfing competition was back on. Not only was the need to get back out on the water strong simply because that was what she loved doing, but now she knew she needed to familiarise herself with her new board if she was to have any chance of placing high enough in the championship to earn a cash prize.

And what was she doing instead? Hanging around outside an old man's house waiting to find out if he was going to let them in or not.

The wind tugged at Eden's hair and clothing, reminding her that the weather conditions were changing.

Finally they heard the bolt being thrown back and keys rattling. The door opened a crack, and Simeon peeped through the narrow gap.

'Hello Simeon,' Jim said. 'I'm really sorry to bother you, but would you mind if we popped in for five minutes?'

'I've already had visitors today, Jim,' the old man said. Eden was surprised at the soft sound of his voice. She wasn't sure what she had been expecting, a wizened old cackle or something, but not this gentle voice.

'I know, and I'm sorry,' Jim replied.

'But it's those visitors we've come to talk about.'

Simeon's eyes darted from Jim to Finn and then to Eden, and finally back to Jim again.

'All right, just for a minute,' he said, opening the door wider.

They stepped into the dark, musty-smelling hall, and to Eden it was like walking back in time. The old-fashioned, floral paper was curling at the edges where damp was peeling it from the walls. A very threadbare carpet covered the floor.

Simeon led them into the front room. There was a single armchair, a table beside it on which lay a newspaper and a stained mug of half-finished tea on it. An old-fashioned television set sat in the corner.

The black cat was still perched on the windowsill, staring balefully at the newcomers.

Simeon sat down in the single chair. He reached out for his mug of tea and Eden noticed a tremor in his hand.

'Did they tell you who they were, these visitors?' Jim said.

Simeon sipped noisily at his tea.

'Lawyers, they said they were lawyers.'

'How many of them were there?'

'Three, two men and a woman. All in their fancy suits and with their fancy ways.'

'And what did they want?' Jim asked.

Simeon took another noisy slurp of tea.

'They wanted me to admit to trespassing, and to causing that leak by damaging one of their outlets with the hull of my boat. They said if I made a statement, if I admitted it, they wouldn't charge me for the repairs and the clean-up.'

'What did you say?' Eden asked. She had intended to keep her mouth shut, let Jim do all the talking, but seeing this vulnerable, lonely old man and hearing how he had been intimidated by powerful lawyers working for an even more powerful company, she couldn't help but speak. 'Did you admit it?'

Simeon stared at Eden and there was a fire in his eyes, a bright hot defiance. 'Of course not. I didn't do what they said, so why should I take the blame for it? I never go anywhere near their stinking building, there's no fishing to be had there anyway.'

'So why do they think the damage and the leak is your fault?' Jim said.

Simeon turned to look at Jim, and Eden felt a sense of relief wash over her. For a vulnerable old man, he certainly had a powerful stare.

'Because it's their cock-up, but they need someone to take the blame,' Simeon said. 'They punched a hole in the bottom of my boat, made it look like I had a collision. They're framing me.'

'What did they say when you told them you weren't going to admit you're at fault?' Jim said.

'They told me they would be prosecuting me for the cost of repairs, lost profits and the cost of the clean-up in the sea. They said I would spend the rest of my life paying for it.'

Simeon put his mug of tea on the side table, pulled a handkerchief out of his pocket and began dabbing at his eyes. Eden looked at Jim and Finn. They appeared to be as shocked as she felt.

Jim cleared his throat.

'Don't worry, Simeon, it won't come to that.'

'And how do you know that?' Simeon said.

'Because we won't let it happen,' Eden said. 'You have friends here, and no one's going to let these bullies try and walk all over you.'

Simeon sighed. His head was bowed, his hands lying in his lap. He looked small and helpless.

Jim glanced at Eden and Finn. 'Let's go.'

They said their goodbyes to Simeon and let themselves out. Eden blinked in the bright sunshine.

'You were right,' she said to Finn. 'Max Charon was lying.'

'It helps that I've known my Uncle

Max all my life. Lying is his default position. And did you notice how the stories didn't even tie up? Uncle Max said Simeon's anchor got caught in a cable and caused the damage, but those lawyers told him it was the hull of his boat.'

'What do we do now?' Eden said.

'I'm going to pay Uncle Max another visit,' Finn said. 'And I'm going to lay it on the line, everything we found out today. This needs to stop.'

'I'll come with you,' Eden said.

Finn shook his head. 'No — this time I'm going on my own. It could get unpleasant and I don't want you getting dragged into it.'

'I think he's right,' Jim said. 'Come back to the workshop — I'll put the kettle on.'

Eden grimaced. 'I'm sorry, Jim, you know I love you, and you're the world's number one when it comes to making surfboards, but your coffee and tea-making?' She held up her hands. 'No way.'

'What's wrong with my coffee and tea?' Jim said, a look of mock horror on his face.

'Uh, like, dishwater!' Eden said. 'Tell you what, we'll head back into town and you can take me somewhere nice and buy me a coffee instead.'

Jim looked at Finn. 'Is this how she treats all her friends, or is it just me?'

Laughing, Finn said, 'Don't drag me into this. Look, I'll catch up with you guys later.'

'Good luck!' Eden called as he walked off. 'Be careful.'

Finn waved and continued walking.

'That's a nice young man you've bagged yourself there,' Jim said, as they watched him walking away.

'Excuse me?' Eden replied.

Jim grinned, that craggy, lopsided grin that Eden loved so much.

'I may be old enough to be your grandad, but that doesn't mean to say I'm going senile. I could see the little glances you were giving each other when you thought no one was looking.

You two are an item, aren't you?'

Eden blushed a little and dropped her eyes.

'I'm really happy,' Jim said. 'It's been a long time, too long. You deserve this.'

Eden slipped her arm through Jim's.

'Before you get all soppy on me, why don't you walk me into town and buy me that coffee?'

'We're going to turn heads, walking into town like this, an old pensioner like me with a beautiful young woman on his arm.'

'Is that a problem?'

Jim chuckled. 'Not at all.'

# 7

For the first time in a long time, Eden felt happy and relaxed. This was a revelation to her, as she had spent the last five years thinking she was content, living her life on her terms, her way. But these last two days had changed everything.

Having Finn in her life suddenly seemed to show up the emptiness of her previous existence. Where she had thought she was being strong and independent, she now wondered if perhaps she had been lonely. She just hadn't realised it.

*Slow down, Eden*, she told herself as these and more thoughts rushed through her mind. *You've only just met Finn, and the way you're going on you'll be proposing to him tomorrow. Take it easy.*

The two of them hardly knew each other. But not only was Eden happy, all her friends were happy for her too. Had she really cut such a lonely figure on the surfing scene?

Maybe.

Right now, though, she needed to get her focus back on the surfing championships. All this relationship malarkey, not to mention the hideous plastic pollution, was messing with her focus. Eden needed to go out on the water with her new board and get to know it.

Finn had taken the pressure off her finances by buying her a new surfboard, but the reality remained that she had no money and she needed to win one of the cash prizes on offer if she was to keep her lifestyle.

All these thoughts and more passed through her head as she sat in the Wave cafe. Jim had bought a black Americano for her and a latte for him. They chatted and laughed and people-watched until Jim finally had to leave and get back to the workshop.

Eden had stayed sitting at the table,

lost in her thoughts until she was interrupted.

And her world came crashing down again.

'Excuse me? It's Eden, right? Eden Hawks?'

Eden looked up. 'Yes.'

The man standing by her table was dressed in a shirt and tie, but that didn't make him look smart or well presented. His collar was undone and his tie pulled loose. His shirt was hanging out of his trousers in places. A tousled mop of greying hair, spectacles repaired with sticky tape, and stubble covering his chin and cheeks, finished the unkempt appearance off.

'Tom Maddox,' he said, holding out an ink-stained hand.

'You say that as though it should mean something to me,' Eden said, ignoring the hand.

'No, of course not, of course you don't know me,' he said, a little flustered. 'That's why I'm here, sort of. Um, do you mind if I sit down?'

'I don't suppose I can stop you,' Eden said, coldly.

Maddox had a brown paper parcel clutched under his arm, held together with wide, green parcel tape. The paper was falling apart, though, and Eden could see sheaves of typed pages peeking out of the torn corners. He put the parcel on the table and took a seat opposite Eden.

He took his glasses off and polished the lenses with his tie. When he put them back on, he smiled sheepishly at Eden, then glanced around.

'I don't think they do table service here. You have to order from the counter,' Eden said.

'Oh, right, of course,' Maddox said. 'Do you mind if I . . . ?' He pointed at the serving counter.

Eden shook her head.

'Can I get you anything?' he said.

Eden shook her head again.

Maddox got up and left her alone. He also left his tatty, brown paper parcel on the table.

Some rips in the parcel were quite big, and Eden could see portions of the upside-down type quite clearly. She glanced up and saw Maddox busy at the till, his back to her. Turning her attention back to the parcel, she promised herself she wasn't going to look at it. Whatever was in there was no business of hers.

She glanced up again. Maddox was still busy at the till.

Eden leaned forward a little, staring at the upside down type revealed to her through a rip in the brown paper wrapping.

And she made out the words *Charon Recycling*.

Eden sat back in her chair as Maddox bustled back, pushing his glasses back up his nose, holding a mug of milky tea.

'You know, I've got places to be,' Eden said, pushing her chair back and getting ready to stand up. 'I didn't invite you to sit down and talk to me, and whatever it is you want from me, I suggest you forget all about it.'

Maddox stared at Eden, his mouth hanging open like a fly trap.

'I'm pretty sure I know who you are,' Eden said. 'You and your colleagues should be ashamed of yourselves, bullying a lonely old man like that.'

'I don't know what you're talking about, you're mistaking me for someone else,' Maddox said.

Eden had been about to stand up, but she paused. 'You're not one of those lawyers?'

'I don't know which lawyers you're talking about,' Maddox said. 'But I'm a reporter, so I suppose I'm not.'

Eden relaxed back into her seat. 'A reporter?'

'Yes, I'm with the South Cornwall Gazette.'

Maddox fumbled in his trouser pockets and finally pulled out a lanyard, all tied up in knots, with a reporter's pass on the end. A faded photograph of a younger-looking, but unmistakable, Maddox was laminated on the creased, battered card.

Maddox stuffed the identity card back in his pocket, leaving loops of the lanyard hanging out. He took a slurp of his tea and smiled at Eden.

'So what do you want with me?' Eden said.

'Charon Recycling,' Maddox tapped his parcel. 'I think we're both on the same side, aren't we?'

'That depends whose side you're on.'

Maddox's eyes widened behind his glasses, the lenses magnifying them to comical proportions.

'The side of truth and honesty, of course!'

'Can you just tell me what you want? I wasn't joking when I said I had a busy day, and at this rate we're still going to be here tomorrow morning.'

Maddox pushed his glasses back into place once more. 'Yes, yes, of course.' He paused, and the expression on his face almost seemed sly to Eden. 'A little bird tells me you paid Max Charon a visit earlier today.'

'Oh, really?' Eden leaned forward.

'And what little bird was that?'

'Ah, I'm afraid, ah, I'm afraid that would be divulging my sources and I can't do that.'

Eden leaned forward a little more. 'What do you want with me, Mr Maddox?'

Maddox smiled. 'I want the same thing as you, Eden. I want to expose Max Charon for the criminal he is, and protect our beautiful, Cornish coastline.'

Eden relaxed back into her chair again.

'Oh, I see.'

'Do you?' Maddox said, pushing his glasses up the ridge of his nose. 'Max Charon is a very clever, sly, weaselly little man. I've been after him for over two years now, but he's a slippery fellow, and every time I think I have him he slides out of my grasp.'

Maddox held a fist up and as he said these last words, he opened it and wriggled his fingers, as though letting something loose.

Eden shifted in her seat. Maddox was

an odd man, for sure, but if he was out to bring Charon down and put a stop to the poisoning of the coastline, he would be a definite ally.

'So what do you want from me?' Eden said.

The reporter leaned in close and looked around the cafe.

'Listen, this is important. You need to be careful.' His voice dropped to a whisper. 'I have a mole on the inside.'

'A mole?' Eden said. 'On the inside?'

'Yes, yes, that's what I said.'

'Do you think maybe you should see a doctor?' Eden said.

Maddox looked a little perplexed for a moment, and then his face cleared. 'No, no, not that kind of mole. The other kind. In Charon Recycling.'

Now Eden immediately thought of the animal, and she had to suppress a giggle at the thought of a mole in Charon Recycling. Moles, sharks, what next? Tigers? Elephants? Perhaps Uncle Max was a latter-day Noah, preparing for the end of the world. Come to think of it, there was a storm on the way. It all fitted.

Eden pushed these ridiculous thoughts from her head.

'You mean a spy, don't you?' she said.

'Yes, yes, a spy! Someone on the inside, someone who's reporting back to me.' He patted the brown paper parcel. 'He's the one who gave me all these.'

'Are they confidential documents?' Eden said.

Maddox nodded. 'Oh yes, very confidential.'

'What do they say?' Eden was eager to know more.

'Oh, I can't tell you, I'm afraid they're confidential,' Maddox said.

'You already told me that,' Eden sighed. 'What was the point of bringing them here to me if you're not going to show them to me?'

Maddox took another slurp of his tea, and some of it slopped onto the table.

*He really is quite disgusting*, Eden thought. *I bet he lives on his own.*

'You need to be careful,' Maddox said.

'You already told me that too,' Eden said. 'Do you get the feeling we're going around in circles?'

Like that shark, in Charon's glorified fish tank.

'My mole,' Maddox said, his voice dropping even lower, 'he told me there's another mole.'

'Another mole? Wow. One more and you'll have a labour.'

Maddox, lifting his mug of tea to his mouth, stopped and gazed at Eden. 'A labour?'

'Yes, a group of moles is called a labour. One more mole, because I'm not sure two moles counts as a group, and you will have a labour of moles inside Charon's Lab.'

Maddox looked even more perplexed, then the confusion cleared. 'Ah! No! This second mole, he's not in the lab, he's outside.'

'But what good is that?' Eden said. 'How can he provide you with top secret documents and stuff if he's not in the lab?'

'Because he's not working for us, that's why.'

*Us?* thought Eden. *Since when did we suddenly become a team?*

'He's working for Max Charon,' Maddox continued. 'That's why I want you to be careful.'

'I don't understand,' Eden said. 'If he's a mole, and he's working for Charon, then . . .'

'That's right, he's pretending to be one of you, pretending to be a surfer.'

A cold hand clutched Eden's heart and squeezed. 'Do we know this mole's name?'

'Oh yes,' Maddox said, sliding his glasses back up the ridge of his nose. 'It's Max Charon's nephew — Finn.'

# 8

Eden struggled to believe what Maddox had told her. Surely he had got it wrong? Or, more likely, his man on the inside — his mole — had got it wrong.

Finn couldn't be a traitor. Eden might have known him only a day or two, but she felt that they had connected with each other.

He couldn't be secretly working for Max Charon.

Could he?

After all, Finn had tried hiding his connection with his Uncle Max from Eden and the others. Why had he done that? Was it really because of his embarrassment with the family name? Or a more sinister reason?

And what about his surfing ability? As far as Eden knew, no one had seen him in the water yet. Eden had, but he'd done what no reasonably experienced surfer should have, and gone into the water far too close to her own surfing spot.

Perhaps even that had been nothing more than a ruse, a way of meeting Eden and wriggling his way into the group?

But it all seemed so ridiculous. They weren't children, playing at secret agents and spies. This wasn't the world of James Bond, with a dastardly villain to face who was attempting to take over the entire world.

Even if, Eden had to admit, Max Charon looked a little like a James Bond villain in his underground lair with his great white shark. All he was missing was a white cat sitting on his lap for him to stroke.

Or maybe a mole . . .

*Ah, Miss Hawks, I have been expecting you.*

Yes, that was how silly all this was beginning to sound. Tom Maddox had it wrong. The way he had talked, he had made everything sound so sinister. But he hadn't given her any specifics.

Besides, what harm could a plastic recycling plant be up to? There needed to be more initiatives like this if humanity was going to clean up the planet for future generations.

And yet, Charon Recycling were now responsible for an environmental disaster themselves. And their track record had been pretty bad before this — so bad, in fact, that their name was mud among environmentalists. Toxic mud.

Eden dropped her head into her hands and groaned. Her thoughts were racing, bumping against each other, shooting off in different directions.

She lay down on her bunk bed and closed her eyes. After leaving Maddox at the cafe, Eden had hurried straight back to the youth hostel and up to her room. She didn't know what to do next.

Maddox had told her she mustn't let anyone know about Finn, not for the time being at least. He'd said that the more people who knew about the traitor in their midst, the more likely there would be a slip-up and that Finn would find out.

'We have to keep this knowledge between ourselves,' Maddox had said.

'I'm still not sure I believe it,' Eden protested. 'Isn't there a way we can find out for sure?'

Maddox had hatched a plan. Eden would feed Finn false information, maybe something to do with the protests against Charon Labs, then Maddox would check with his mole. If the mole found out that same information from Max Charon, he could only have received it from Finn.

Which would mean Finn was a traitor.

Eden had reluctantly agreed, and they had cooked up a lie between them to tell Finn.

Eden hated the thought of lying to Finn, but if it cleared his name, then it would be worth it.

And now here she was, back at the youth hostel, waiting for Finn to return from his meeting with his Uncle Max. She felt sick to her stomach.

Eden heard voices and clattering from downstairs. The others were back, but was Finn among them? Eden knew she had to go downstairs at some point, but she put the moment off. How could she face him without giving herself away? Surely one glance, one moment looking into her eyes, and Finn would know something was wrong.

There had to be a way around that. Maybe if she pretended she was upset about their visit to Simeon earlier? That was true, she was upset. How anyone could treat an old, defenceless man in that way was beyond her understanding.

Eden took a deep breath and sat up. It was time to go downstairs and face Finn.

And lie to him.

*But you have to tell him that lie*, she told herself. *By doing this you will be clearing Finn's name.*

But what if Maddox was right? What if Finn was betraying them? What if he was nothing like the man Eden thought he was?

152

Well, she would be devastated. But that didn't mean she should lie to herself, pretend everything was fine. She needed to know the truth. They all did.

But still she sat there, on the edge of the bed, reluctant to move.

She looked at the paper shark on the windowsill and thought about Max Charon clipping at its edges with those long, black-handled scissors. He had been so precise, yet so gentle with the paper model. A delicate replica of a predatory killing machine. The contrast between the two seemed to hold true of the man himself. Someone whose words were so silky and smooth, who talked of doing the right thing and could make beautiful paper structures like that shark, and yet Eden sensed a steely ruthlessness in him, a cruel streak.

The sound of laughter floated upstairs. They were in good spirits, despite everything.

*Come on, get yourself in gear*, Eden thought. *It will all be fine. It will. It has to be.*

She stood up and opened her door. The laughter grew louder. She glanced back into her room, at the paper shark sitting on her windowsill.

'Wish me luck, Bruce,' she whispered.

She took a deep breath and headed downstairs.

They were all there, in the kitchen, including Finn. All smiles and laughter.

'Hey!' Larry said, seeing Eden in the doorway. 'We were wondering where you'd got to.'

Eden shrugged and forced a smile. 'I was in my room, I went for a lie down and I fell asleep.'

'Are you all right?' Finn said, walking over to her and slipping a hand into hers.

Eden smiled up at him. The smile felt horribly forced, more like a grimace. She felt exposed in front of him, as if he could see every thought and feeling, like he must already know that she was about to lie to him.

'I'm just tired,' she said. 'Tired and upset.'

154

The others looked at her, all hilarity extinguished.

'Has something happened?' Larry asked.

Eden shook her head as Finn gave her hand a gentle squeeze. 'No, it's just . . . has Finn told you about our visit to see Simeon?'

Larry nodded. 'Yeah.'

'I just find it so hard to believe that anyone could treat an old man like that. This will crush him if Charon prosecutes Simeon.'

'Hey, you know we're going to look after him?' Finn said. 'Remember, Jim told him that.'

Eden nodded, wiping a hand across her eyes. She was crying for real, and was glad of this cover story about Simeon to blame her tears on.

'Hey, how did it go with your uncle?' she said, letting go of Finn's hand and sitting down at the table. She clasped her hands and stared at them. Anything to avoid looking Finn in the eye.

'Not good,' Finn said, sitting down

next to her. The others joined them at the table, the mood now subdued. 'Uncle Max was in no mood to talk — in fact I didn't think I was going to get to see him at all at first.'

'Was Jagger there?' Eden asked.

'Yes, he was there, and when I finally made it down to Uncle Max's office —'

'The one where he has a great white in captivity, amongst other species?' Nina said.

'Yeah, that's the one,' Finn said. 'Well, when I got down there Uncle Max and Jagger were waiting for me, and right away they just laid into me about how I should come back to the family business, how I was betraying them and the family name by hanging out with losers.'

'They called us losers?' Doug shouted. 'Why, I oughtta —'

'Calm down,' Ellie said, placing a hand on Doug's shoulder. 'Let's hear Finn's story.'

'Well, they barraged me with reasons for why I should ditch the surfer lifestyle and come back to work with them. Most, actually all, the reasons were just emotional blackmail.'

'I don't understand,' Eden said. 'Jagger told you never to return when he showed us out. He said you were an embarrassment to the family.'

'I know, but I think that's just Jagger being two-faced. He knows his dad wants me back and, even though Jagger would rather I stayed away he daren't reveal that to Uncle Max for fear of being demoted or losing his inheritance. Uncle Max can be pretty explosive if he feels offended.'

'It couldn't have been pleasant for you down there, all by yourself,' Larry said.

'No, it wasn't,' Finn admitted. 'And when I got on to confronting them about Simeon, and how they were setting up to ruin him, it got even more unpleasant. Jagger got so red in the face I thought he was going to punch me.'

'Couldn't you persuade them to see sense at all?' Nina said.

'Unfortunately not,' Finn said. 'They basically repeated what Simeon told us, that if Simeon admitted to trespassing and causing the damage that released the plastic waste, then Charon would foot the bill for the clean-up and the repairs. But if he refused to take responsibility . . .'

Larry pounded the table with his fist. 'It's just so unfair! Simeon can't afford to take this to court and fight it!'

'He might be able to,' Eden said.

'How?' Doug said. 'The old guy's a penniless fisherman.'

Eden girded herself for the lie. A lie she was telling not only to Finn, but all of her friends gathered in this room. The thought of lying to them made her feel ill. But she had to do it; she'd agreed with Maddox that this was the only way of finding out whose side Finn was on.

'I met a reporter from a local newspaper earlier today,' Eden said. 'He told me that if it goes to court, they are prepared to put up the money for a defence fund. He said they will also be asking for donations. Apparently they have already spoken to a lawyer who thinks they could win any case brought against Simeon by Charon Labs.'

'That is good news,' Larry said, sighing with relief.

'When are they announcing that?' Finn said.

Was it Eden's imagination, or had his tone of voice gone a notch cooler?

'They're not, at the moment,' Eden replied. 'They want us to keep it a secret, I shouldn't even have told you lot, but I couldn't keep it to myself. They won't say anything until they find out what Charon Recycling are going to do.'

'That doesn't make sense,' Doug said. 'Shouldn't they be announcing it now to try and put Charon off?'

'I don't know.' Eden shrugged. 'I just know Maddox told me not to mention it to anyone.'

'Well, at least it's something,' Nina said.

They all sat in silence for a while. The silence continued until Finn stood up and stretched.

'I'm going to head out for a walk, it's been a long day,' he said. 'I need some fresh air.'

Eden thought about saying she would go with him, but she was terrified of giving herself away. She said nothing, even when Finn looked at her as though silently asking her if she was coming.

'I'll catch up with you later,' she said, briefly giving him eye contact, then quickly looking away.

'Alright,' Finn said, his tone seeming to say he wasn't sure what was going on.

Eden said nothing, just watched as Finn left.

Silence fell over the group once more, until Doug finally spoke up, and said, 'Hey, you know what? We should have a party tonight.'

'Are you serious?' Larry yelled. 'What is it with you and parties? Don't you realise we have championships the day after tomorrow?'

'Yeah? So what? We've got plenty of time to rest before then.'

'You're unbelievable,' Larry said, laughing.

Ellie draped her arm over Doug's shoulders and kissed him. 'My man, he just likes to party.'

'Doesn't everyone?' Doug said.

★ ★ ★

Eden decided to go and find Finn after all, catch up with him and join him in his walk. She knew she was being irrational, that her mind and her heart were jumping from trusting him to believing he was a liar. If she carried on like this for much longer, she felt as though she would explode.

But what could she do? She was tempted to tell Finn the truth about her meeting with Maddox, about what he had said, and the lie they had cooked up together. But what would that solve?

Of course Finn would deny everything, whether he was guilty or innocent.

161

And Eden would never truly be rid of the sneaking suspicion that Maddox had planted within her.

Why did this have to be so complicated? All she wanted to do was surf. That was all she had ever wanted. And she had thought that was all she would ever want.

But her life was changing. Finn had changed it, and for the better.

Except maybe not . . .

Eden stopped her jog along the coastal path, tilted her head back and screamed. By the time she had finished she felt a little better.

But not much.

She started running along the path once more. Finn could have gone anywhere, but Eden had taken a gamble he would have followed his usual route. The wind buffeted her and tugged at her clothing as she ran. A reminder that a storm was building out at sea and headed their way.

Eden arrived at the cove where they had dunked each other in the sea. The plastic pollution seemed even heavier now, as though the tanks full of waste plastic at Charon Recycling were still emptying. How much plastic were they recycling? And what were they doing with it all?

The beach was empty. Eden's heart ached at the sight of it. She had thought he would be here, waiting for her. But no. Wherever he had gone, she wouldn't find him now.

Had he done it on purpose? Was he avoiding her now? Or even worse, had he gone straight back to his Uncle Max, to tell him the news?

To repeat the lie that Eden had just fed him?

As the cold wind whipped around her, tugging at her clothes and hair, Eden wiped at the tears rolling down her cheeks.

# 9

The next morning, Eden woke so early that it was still dark. The party, to Doug's disappointment, hadn't gone ahead last night after all.

Nobody was in the mood, and with the surfing championships back on, everyone wanted to rest and keep fresh. There was no way they were going to let Doug dupe them into drinking and partying hard less than forty-eight hours before a major competition.

Eden dressed quickly, ate two bananas for a quick burst of energy, then padded down the stairs where she stumbled across Finn in the kitchen, eating a bowl of porridge.

'There's more in the pan,' he said, pointing at the cooker and grinning.

'What are you doing up?' Eden said.

'I thought we could go surfing,' Finn said, through a mouthful of porridge.

'We?' Eden said, raising an eyebrow, but giving him a smile too.

'And I promise to come nowhere near you in the water,' Finn said. 'I don't want you shoving me in the chest again, that hurt.'

'It did not!' Eden replied.

'Well, maybe only a little.' Finn scooped up the last of his porridge. 'You having any?'

Eden shook her head. 'I've eaten two bananas.'

Finn put his bowl in the sink. 'You ready then?'

Eden couldn't make sense of her emotions. Last night she had gone to bed early, not wanting to be around Finn with the others. If the two of them had been on their own, she might have opened up to him, talked about the accusation Maddox had made. But she couldn't do that in front of her friends.

Eden had spent a restless night tossing and turning, her sleep plagued with nightmares. In one particularly frightening dream, the world's plastic had covered all the oceans and fused together, trapping the sea beneath its surface. No one could swim or surf or sail in it any more.

When she had finally woken up she had been tired, but determined to find somewhere clear of plastic pollution where she could surf.

She needed to get back out on the water. Not just to familiarise herself with her new board, or for the practice she needed for the upcoming championships, but to clear her head. The surfing always did that for her; it was an act of meditation.

But she had intended going on her own. And now here Finn was, offering to go with her.

What reason could she give for saying no? That would surely draw suspicion down on her. Eden resigned herself to the thought that she had to go along with this. She had to pretend everything was fine between them. At least until Maddox got back to her later today, and either confirmed or denied what his mole had told him.

With a huge mental and emotional effort, Eden squashed her tangle of emotions deep inside, smiled at Finn, and said, 'I'm ready, let's go.'

They closed the hostel's front door quietly behind them, and ran across the car park to Selina the camper van.

'I know of a place we can go,' Finn said, as they stashed their gear in the back. 'It should be clear of any plastic, and it's quiet too.'

They climbed into the camper van and Finn turned the ignition key, Selina's engine rumbling into life. Despite the turmoil of yesterday and last night's dreams, Eden's insides were now alive with excitement and anticipation.

Finn drove out of the carpark. Thankfully for Eden, he didn't seem to be in a mood for talking just yet. Maybe it was that time of the morning, when it seemed perfectly sensible to whisper, even if there was no reason to do so. Being up and about so early had a sense of reverence about it, as though they were in a cathedral.

Selina's headlights illuminated their way as they navigated the twists and turns of the narrow country lanes. Finn had to brake sharply at one point as two rabbits scampered across the road.

'They're so cute!' Eden whispered as she watched them disappear into the hedge at the side of the road.

'But look at that,' Finn said. 'Now that's truly beautiful.'

Eden lifted her eyes and drank in the sight of the horizon as it slowly lit up in a glow of orange and red. The camper van had come to a stop at the brow of a hill, and it was a perfect spot for them to look out across the sea.

'The weather has cleared,' Eden said.

'You're right. I hadn't even noticed.'

The wind had died down, and the clouds broken up, their edges tinged with the colour of fire. The first rays of the sun broke across the horizon. The tips of the waves looked as though they were dancing with flames.

'Looks like the storm has passed us

by after all,' Finn said.

'Thank goodness,' Eden sighed. 'Now we can get on with the surfing championships.'

*And maybe it's a sign,* Eden thought. *A sign that everything's going to be fine, after all.*

'Come on,' she said. 'What are waiting for?'

Finn laughed. Selina's engine rumbled and rattled as they began their steep descent down the narrow lane towards the sea. Hedges and trees closed in on either side, and the sea disappeared and reappeared on each bend.

The narrow lane opened out into a basic car park, full of potholes and scattered gravel. Selina bounced up and down as Finn did his best to avoid the deepest potholes. He parked up facing the sea and switched the engine off.

They sat and gazed at the ocean, at the waves crashing onto the deserted beach. Apart from the ticking of the cooling engine, the only sound was the surf.

'It looks perfect,' Finn whispered.

'Let's go,' Eden said, eager to get in the sea and riding the waves crashing against the beach and the rocky headland. They pulled their boards out of the van and walked down the winding steps.

Standing on the cool, damp sand, they faced the ocean's raw power as the waves cascaded against the shore. A surge of relief flushed Eden's body and mind as she looked at the sea unspoilt by plastic waste.

Her stomach tingled with the anticipation of riding the waves — not harnessing their power but going with it, letting the flow take over.

'Isn't it amazing?' murmured Finn.

'Beautiful,' Eden replied.

She began walking towards the sea, her surfboard under her arm. She didn't want to talk any more, didn't want to stand and admire the sea's beauty any longer. She needed to be in it.

Picking up the pace, Eden began

running. The waves crashed against her legs as she waded into the cold water. Pulling the board from under her arm and gripping the edges, she threw herself onto her surfboard against an incoming wave. The seawater frothed over her, flushing away the last remains of sleep from her body.

She surfaced, her new board carrying her up and out of the water, and she laughed. This was her life, this was everything. To find that moment, to live fully in it, was the only way she could feel alive and free.

Eden didn't pause to look behind and see if Finn had followed her. He was on his own now, as was she. They each had to find their own relationship with the sea, commune with it, ask for its permission to spend time within its environment, and to respect it.

Eden, still lying face down on the board, paddled with her hands. The ocean's swell lifted and then lowered her, revealing the horizon to her and then hiding it as she plunged down between the peaks of the ocean's rolling mounds of water.

When she found the right spot, she turned the board around to face the shoreline once more and sat up, legs dangling in the water. Finn was nowhere to be seen, but he would be out there, on the water. Preferably out of her way this time.

For this was her moment. Just her and her new board. Above her the sky, turning lighter with every passing second. Below her the sea, filled with mystery and power.

And Eden, caught in between, waiting for that moment to harness the power of nature, and soar.

She glanced behind at the oncoming waves. One of them looked perfect for what she needed. She had to time this just right.

Eden lay down on her front again and began paddling, pulling at the water, urging her board along. The swell of the moving water carried her with it. This was the critical moment, when she and her board and the ocean had to become one. To coexist for the next few seconds.

And there it was, that magical moment where a pair of invisible hands lifted her board, gave her flight over the water. Eden jumped up onto one knee, then up onto both feet. A wall of water rose behind her as her board picked up speed. The sound of rushing water, the elemental power of the wave, filled her ears. Eden was lost to all conscious thought, existing purely on an instinctual level. Living for that moment alone.

Filled with joy, Eden yelled and whooped. She adjusted her position as the power of the wave changed. The beach was much closer and she could hear the sea crashing against the sand, hissing and foaming. She changed position slightly, angling the board towards the shoreline.

Within moments she was gliding on the depleting power of the wave, her wave, onto the beach. She jumped off the board. Knee-deep in the water, she looked up and down the beach until she found Finn.

He was sitting on the sand next to his board. He lifted an arm and waved at her.

'Hey, that was great!' he yelled.

Eden grinned. 'Wasn't it?'

Picking her board up, she walked up the beach and flopped down next to him.

'You looked amazing out there,' Finn said. 'How's the new board?'

Eden placed a hand on it, almost caressing it like a dear friend.

'Fantastic. It's like I've always owned it, and I already know all its quirks and subtleties.'

'Jim said he'd made it specially for you,' Finn replied.

'Yeah, he's amazing,' Eden said. She looked at Finn, cross-legged on the sand, making no move to get in the water. 'Aren't you going out?'

He grimaced. 'No, I can't. Look.'

Finn tilted his surfboard upright on

its side. Running halfway down its length was a hairline crack, zigzagging along its surface.

'Oh no!' Eden said. 'How did that happen?'

Finn laid his board back down on the sand. 'I don't know. I just noticed it when we got down to the beach and I was getting ready to follow you into the sea.'

'Does this mean you can't compete?'

'Not unless I get a new board pretty fast.'

Eden looked out across the waves. She was going back in very soon. She had to. She had to get away, lose herself on the waves once more.

Because tendrils of unease were creeping up her spine and into her mind and her gut. A thought had struck her, just at that moment.

She hadn't seen Finn surfing once. And now she had to ask herself, did he even know how?

If what Maddox said was true, that Finn was spying on Eden and the others for Max Charon, then would he know how to surf? Probably not; he probably spent most of his time in board-rooms at meetings, or on business calls.

He looked the part of a surfer. He was in shape, for starters. Didn't that count for something?

*He could have got that body in the gym though*, that voice of unease said quietly.

What about his long hair, and his tan? Surely they were indicators of the lifestyle he led.

*Two weeks on holiday in a sunny, hot country would have given him a tan. And it doesn't take that long to grow your hair out.*

Eden clenched her fists and ground her teeth. This was meant to be a chance for her to relax, out on the waves. Instead she was on the beach, growing more tense with each passing moment.

Maybe there was a chance to answer this question one way or another, right now.

'Why don't you take my board out?' she said.

'I couldn't do that,' Finn said. 'She's yours, Jim made her for you.'

'No, really, I'd love to see you out there,' Eden replied. 'Go on, take my board — let's see what you've got.'

Finn looked at her quizzically.

'You're in the championships, right?' Eden said. 'I want to see what I'll be up against.'

'Seriously, that's a great offer, but no,' Finn replied, laughing. 'I really don't want to risk damaging your board, and besides, I need to keep some secrets to myself.'

*Looks that way*, Eden thought, sadly.

Jumping to her feet and picking up her surfboard, she said, 'Right, I'm going back in!'

She ran to the water's edge and threw herself into the waves. Anything to try and wash away the tension and the unhappiness gripping her mind and emotions.

★ ★ ★

Eden had expected the others would be out by the time her and Finn returned to the youth hostel. She had thought they would be surfing, preparing for the championship. But no, everyone was sitting around the large kitchen table.

And there was someone new. Not a surfer, that much was obvious. His skin was pasty white — it looked as if this might be the first time in his life he had stepped outside. And he wasn't built like a surfer. Eden knew there were all body shapes and sizes out on the water, and that some of the most dedicated surfers of all still didn't have six packs and arms like tree trunks. But everyone who surfed regularly looked fit and strong — even if they didn't fit the classic, stereotyped image displayed in films and adverts.

This guy just looked out of shape.

'Here they are!' Larry said. 'We've been waiting for you.'

'What's going on?' Eden said, sitting down next to Nina and gazing at the newcomer.

Finn sat down as well, next to Doug.

'Say hi to Billy,' Larry said.

'Hi Billy,' Eden and Finn said at the same time.

Billy glanced nervously at them. He was chewing on a thumbnail. He didn't look too happy.

'Billy, now that Eden and Finn are here, why don't you tell us your news?' Larry said.

Billy mumbled something, still chewing his nail.

'What was that?' Eden said.

Billy looked at her and dropped his hand from his mouth. 'I shouldn't be here.'

He started chewing on his nail again.

Eden looked quizzically at Larry.

'Billy works for Charon Recycling,' Larry said. 'If they find out he's come to see us, it could mean his job.'

'Have you got something you need to tell us?' Finn said.

Had Eden imagined it, or had there been a hint of coldness about Finn's voice? A cruel undercurrent she had never heard before?

Billy shook his head and then changed his mind and nodded. But still he said nothing, just kept on chewing on his thumbnail.

Larry gave Eden a look. She wasn't exactly sure what it meant, but she could see the frustration in his face. And her four friends were all still in pyjamas, hair tousled, eyes sleepy.

Had Billy woken them up and got them out of bed? How long had he been here?

'Why don't I make us all a hot drink?' Ellie said, standing up. 'Billy, would you like a drink?'

Billy hesitated, then said, 'Tea, please. Milky. Three sugars.'

Ellie busied herself, the sounds of the cups and mugs clinking as she arranged them, and the kettle boiling, breaking the uncomfortable silence that had fallen over the group.

Eden's stomach churned at the sight of Billy. If he worked for Charon Recycling and he'd made sure to get here so early so that he wouldn't be spotted and

180

get in trouble, then what he had to say must be important.

Finally, unable to take the silence any longer, Eden said, 'Billy, I can see this is hard for you, that whatever you've got to tell us is difficult and maybe even dangerous. But you're here now, you've made that important step.'

Billy looked at Eden, chewing industriously on his thumbnail.

'It would seem to me that it would be a waste of your time to give up now at the final hurdle, and leave without telling us what you feel we need to know,' Eden continued. 'But if that's what you want to do, nobody here is going to stop you.'

Billy chewed on his thumbnail.

The kettle boiled and switched off.

Billy said, 'I'll tell you.'

Ellie finished making the drinks and passed them around. Billy slurped at his tea.

'I shouldn't be here,' he said again, and looked at everyone, one by one. 'I'm scared. If they find out I'm here, there will be trouble.'

'If who finds out you're here?' Larry said.

'Max Charon, and Jagger.'

'No one's going to tell them, Billy,' Doug said.

Eden had to force herself to remain still, to keep her eyes on Billy. But every instinct in her wanted to turn and look at Finn. If he was a spy for Charon Recycling, as Tom Maddox claimed, then he would betray Billy.

'But people need to know, what they're doing at the factory,' Billy said.

*I should stop him talking now,* Eden thought.

But how? And wasn't it already too late? Even if Billy said nothing more, Finn already knew he was prepared to talk. And he would take that information back to his uncle and cousin.

'Isn't it recycling?' Nina said, leaning forward in her chair, her elbows on the table.

Eden clenched her fists beneath the table.

*Let him talk*, she thought. *It's better that we know what he has come here to tell us.*

'It's recycling, yes,' Billy said, nodding.

'But that's a good thing, isn't it?' Larry said.

Billy shook his head. Eden clenched her teeth to swallow the scream of frustration building inside her chest. Couldn't he just get on with it?

'It should be,' Billy said. 'But it's what they are making with the recycled plastic, that's the problem.'

Eden tipped her head back and let out a groan.

'Please, Billy! What are they making?'

'Weapons,' Billy said. 'They're making weapons.'

# 10

A stunned silence greeted Billy's words. Surely he had to be wrong? How could a recycling company be turning out weapons? Was it even possible?

Eden's eyes flicked involuntarily towards Finn. And he was looking directly at her. What was he thinking? Was he as shocked as the rest of them, or had he already known?

'What do you mean, Billy?' Doug said. 'It's a plastic recycling plant, how can they be making weapons?'

Billy had been chewing on his thumbnail again. With an effort, he pulled his hand away from his mouth. '3D printing. They are using the recycled plastic to print guns and bullets.'

Larry shook his head.

'This just sounds too fantastical to be true.'

'I'm not lying!' Billy said.

'No-one's accusing you of lying,' Larry replied, holding out a placatory hand. 'We just . . . we just want to be sure, that's all.'

'It's true,' Billy said. 'They've already started production on handguns and rifles. They've got advance orders too.'

'Orders from where?' Doug said, quietly.

Billy shrugged. 'Private security firms, arms dealers, black market stuff, you know.'

Eden took a deep breath and unclenched her hands. Had Maddox known any of this? If he did, why hadn't he told her?

'Have you got any proof?' Nina said.

Billy nodded.

'Can we see it?' Larry said.

*This is like sucking blood from a stone*, Eden thought.

Billy nodded. He pulled a mobile from his pocket and used his thumbprint to unlock it. He held the phone out. It displayed a blurred photograph of what looked like a toy handgun lying on a table.

'Is that one of the plastic guns?' Ellie

said, craning her head to look at the photograph.

Billy nodded.

'Have you got a better photo?' Doug said.

Billy shook his head.

'That looks just like a child's toy gun,' Finn said, taking the mobile phone from Billy to have a closer look. 'This doesn't prove a thing.'

Larry looked up at him sharply.

'This is your uncle's company — did you know anything about this?'

'No, of course not,' Finn replied.

'You . . . you're Max Charon's nephew?' Billy had gone whiter than Eden thought was possible. Suddenly he stood up, and his chair fell over with a crash.

'Please, give me my phone back, I should go now,' he said, reaching out to take the mobile from Finn.

'Billy, don't worry. No one here is going to tell Max Charon that you came to see us,' Eden said, not entirely convinced by her own words.

'Sit down, Billy, please,' Nina said.

'No, no, no, no,' Billy muttered. 'I have to go.'

Stuffing the phone back into his pocket, he began pacing the kitchen, seemingly unsure where he should go or how to get out.

*He's a nervous wreck*, thought Eden. *In fact, no, it's worse than that. He's absolutely terrified.*

She glanced at Finn. He had stood up, and he was watching Billy pacing up and down.

Larry was up out of his seat and had his hands on Billy's shoulders. 'Calm down, man, it's OK, you're all right. You're among friends.'

Billy was muttering under his breath and shaking his head, but at least he had stopped pacing.

'Please, come and sit down again,' Ellie said.

Eden glanced at Finn again. He was sitting down again, hands clasped on the table and his head bowed. It seemed as though he was having trouble processing what he had just heard.

'Why are you telling this to us, Billy?' Doug said. 'Don't you think maybe you should be going to the papers?'

'No, no, too dangerous,' Billy muttered, still standing, wringing his hands.

'But why tell us?' Larry said softly. 'What can we do?'

'Wait!' Eden said. 'Are you a spy for a local reporter?'

Billy looked at her, eyes wide and moist. 'No.'

'Then you've got an ally in the company,' Eden said. 'Someone else who knows what is going on and helping expose Max Charon and his company.'

Billy shook his head. 'I don't know . . . I don't know of anyone.'

'That's because they're a spy, silly,' Nina said.

'Come on, sit down, you can have another cup of tea,' Larry said, guiding Billy back to his chair.

'Do you promise not to tell?' Billy said to Finn.

'Cross my heart and hope to die,' Finn said.

188

Billy didn't look convinced, but sat down.

'So come on, Billy, why are you telling this to us?' Larry said. 'What do you think we can do?'

Billy looked down at the table. He couldn't seem to look anyone in the eye. It was as if he was embarrassed now, and he simply wanted to curl up and disappear.

'I've heard about you,' he muttered. 'You're well known for your stance on plastic pollution and cleaning up the environment. I thought you'd want to know.'

'Well, that's nice of you to say so,' Doug said. 'But I really think you should be taking this to the police, or the news stations.'

Billy finally looked up, his face betraying how eager for help he was.

'Can't you do it?' he pleaded. 'I'm not brave enough.'

Larry placed a hand on Billy's shoulder and smiled. 'No one's brave enough, Billy. But sometimes we just need to

189

acknowledge our fear, then do it anyway. You know what I'm saying?'

Billy nodded and lowered his head again.

'I should go now,' he said, his voice suddenly calm. 'I need to get to work. I can't be seen with you.'

'I understand,' Larry said. 'We all do. Go to work, think about what we've said, all right? No-one's forcing you to do anything you don't want to do.'

Billy stood up and wiped his arm over his eyes. Then, without a word, he turned and left.

'Poor guy,' Finn said, watching through the window as Billy walked away.

'Do you think he's telling the truth?' Eden asked.

They were all silent for a moment.

'Yes, I think so,' Larry said. 'But that photo of his isn't the kind of proof we need.'

'Yeah, we need something better than a blurred photo of what looked like a child's toy before we can do anything,' Doug said, and turned to Finn. 'Is there any chance you could go back to dear old cuddly Uncle Max and find us some proof?'

Finn shifted in his chair and grimaced.

'I don't know — we didn't exactly part on the best of terms. And what do I do? Just go right up to him and ask him where he keeps the guns?'

'What else can we do?' Nina said.

'What about your man on the inside?' Larry said to Eden. 'Could he help?'

'He's not my man,' Eden said. 'He's working for this reporter I met. I don't know anything about him.'

'Be interesting to find out who he is,' Finn said.

Eden's heart seemed to stutter to a halt for a moment. Was Finn just curious, like the rest of them? Or did he have a more sinister purpose? Did he want to find out so that he could tell Max Charon? And what about poor Billy? If Finn really was what Maddox claimed, then Billy wasn't safe.

Wait — what was she thinking? Did

she believe Billy was in physical danger if Max Charon found out that he was a whistle-blower?

All of a sudden, Eden pictured the shark swimming round and round in that huge tank, gliding past the large picture window. Its mouth open, revealing those jagged, pointed teeth.

Eden decided she did believe that Billy could be in physical danger, after all. That anyone who opposed the Charons was in danger.

Which meant she had to find out for sure, one way or the other, whose side Finn was on.

And she had to do it soon.

★ ★ ★

The youth hostel had a pay phone in the entrance. Hardly anyone used it, because almost everyone had their own phone. But it still did get used enough that the owner had decided to keep it. Sometimes someone might have run out of credit and need to call home. Or sometimes the mobile phone signal dropped, and then you might find a queue for the public telephone.

But no one ever called in.

Except for this afternoon.

Eden sat in her room, listening to the phone downstairs ringing and ringing. She wondered if someone might answer it, but no one did. She thought about answering it herself, but she didn't want to. She knew who was on the other end.

Instead, she sat on her bed and listened to it ring and tried not to think about Finn.

He'd collared her after Billy left, leaning in close and whispering, 'Can we talk?'

They'd stepped outside. Eden had looked out to sea and wished she was out there, on her surfboard, thinking about nothing other than the waves. The wind pulled and pushed at her, sending her hair flying in all directions. On the horizon she saw dark storm clouds gathering.

It looked as if the storm had changed

its mind about giving South Cornwall a miss. After the beautiful start to the day, the weather was turning nasty.

'Is everything all right?' Finn had said.

He'd taken her by the arm and pulled her closer, but Eden had resisted. Hadn't been able to help herself. She had too many questions, but she was scared to ask them.

'Of course,' she'd said. 'Why do you ask?'

'You just seem . . . off.'

'I'm just worried, you know?' Eden had said. 'This whole situation with Simeon and Charon, it's getting me down.'

Finn had rubbed the side of her arm with his hand. 'I know how you feel. But what can we do?'

'I don't know, but we need to do something! I hate all this sitting around, waiting for something to happen.'

'Maybe things will look better tomorrow,' Finn had said. 'Especially if Simeon gets these lawyers your reporter friend promised.'

Eden hadn't been able to take any more. The lies, the deceit, it was all too much for her.

*Tell him now,* she had thought. *Tell him about Maddox and the lie you both cooked up. Tell him everything and give him a chance to explain.*

Eden had looked up at Finn, looked into his eyes, those deep blue eyes that only yesterday she had been willing to drown herself in, and searched for the truth. Searched for a sign that would tell her, one way or the other, what Finn's true intentions were.

But there was nothing, and all of a sudden Eden lost her nerve. She couldn't tell him about Maddox, she couldn't ask him if what the reporter had told her was true, that he was spying on Eden and her friends. That he was secretly working for his Uncle Max.

'I'm going to my room,' she had said, and turned away, and run back into the Youth Hostel.

The telephone stopped ringing.

195

The sudden silence was jarring, even more unsettling than the ringing had been. Eden held her breath, listening to the muffled voice speaking into the phone, and then the thud of footsteps on the stairs.

Even though she was expecting it, the knock on the door still made her jump.

'Telephone call for you, Eden!' Larry shouted.

'I'll be right down,' Eden called.

There was no way out now. She had to go downstairs and take that call.

Eden hauled herself off the bed and opened her door. She took the stairs slowly, reluctantly. She picked up the telephone off the shelf and put it to her ear.

'Hello?'

'Eden, at long last, it's Tom Maddox.'

'Hi.'

'The news came through from my man on the inside.'

The entrance hall seemed to be growing smaller around Eden, the air getting sucked out. 'Yes?'

'He repeated back to me the lie we cooked up. It's Finn, he's the mole. He's betrayed you all.'

Eden clutched the shelf as her surroundings began to tilt and sway. Finn was working for his uncle. He had no feelings for Eden, he had been using her, manipulating her.

Eden replaced the telephone in the cradle without even saying goodbye.

There was no need to confront Finn any more. She had her answer. All that was left was to tell the others. And she had to do it now, before Finn realised what was happening, that he had been found out.

Eden turned to go and screamed.

Finn had been standing right behind her.

# 11

'Hey, I didn't mean to scare you,' Finn said, reaching out a hand to her.

Eden shrank back. The wall-mounted telephone dug into her back.

'How long have you been there?'

Finn lowered his hand. 'I just got here. You sounded upset, I wanted to know if you were OK.'

'I'm fine,' Eden said.

'Are you sure?'

Eden nodded. She wasn't sure that she could trust herself to speak any more. Her heart thudded in her chest and she had to fight to control her breathing. This was awful — she was hemmed into the corner by Finn.

'Who was that on the telephone?' Finn said. 'You look upset. Has someone upset you?'

'No, honestly, I'm fine,' Eden replied.

'I need to go, I need to go to . . . the toilet!'

She pushed past Finn, shoving him so hard he stumbled a little, and bolted up the stairs and into her room, slamming the door shut behind her.

*You idiot*, she thought. *There are no toilets in the rooms, this is a youth hostel not a five-star hotel.*

Finn would know something was very wrong now. Probably even suspected that his cover was blown. But what would he do?

She needed to tell the others as soon as possible. But there was no way she could leave her room while Finn was hanging around outside.

And what about Billy? Eden kicked herself for having delayed for so long. She should have warned Billy somehow, but it was probably too late now. Finn would already have told his Uncle Max all about the traitor in their company.

There was a soft knock at the door.

'Eden? What's wrong?'

Finn.

'I'm fine,' Eden said. 'I just feel a little ill, I just need to get some sleep, that's all.'

'Eden, I know there's something wrong. Is it me? Have I done something to offend you?'

Eden quickly looked around her room, not even sure what she was looking for. It didn't look as if Finn was about to leave any time soon. But she knew she couldn't sit here in her room while knowing she had led Billy into danger.

If only she wasn't so stubborn about not having a mobile phone!

Eden ran over to the window and opened it. A blast of wind hit her in the face. It picked up the origami shark and sucked it outside, sending it spinning and tumbling in the air.

'Sorry, Bruce,' Eden whispered, watching it fall in a crazy spiral towards the ground. She suddenly felt very sorry for it, and for the shark trapped in Max Charon's glorified aquarium.

Eden decided the ground was too far away for her to jump out of the window.

She was likely to break an ankle at the very least. But there was a drainpipe running down the side of the wall. If she could just reach that, she could shimmy down the pipe. But could she get to it from the window?

Finn knocked on the door again.

'Eden, open up, please. I'm not going anywhere until I find out what this is all about.'

That settled it. She had to make her escape out of the window. She sat on the windowsill and swung her legs out over empty space. She sucked her breath in sharply. The drainpipe was further away than she had realised. Holding on to the side of the window, she stretched out, fingers groping for the plastic pipe. It was maddeningly just out of reach.

The wind whipped her hair across her face, and Eden had to hold on tight to the windowsill, fearful that she would be pulled outside just like Bruce the shark had been.

'Eden, please let me in!'

Finn rattled the door handle and Eden's stomach dropped as she saw the door opening. She had forgotten to lock it! All this time and Finn could have just walked straight into her room.

With no time to waste, Eden threw herself out of the window, around to the side while still hanging on to the window frame with one hand. Her other hand found the drainpipe and her feet smacked against the wall. The drainpipe creaked as she gripped it with both hands, and she heard something snap, but the plastic held.

She slithered down the wall as fast as she could, her trainers scraping against the rough stone and her palms sliding against the plastic drainpipe. When her feet hit the ground, she looked up and saw Finn leaning out the window.

'Eden! What on earth are you doing?'

She turned and ran. Bruce the paper shark was squashed flat under her foot.

She sprinted down the lane towards the village of Covecliff, then took a sharp right onto a coastal footpath. She ran along the twisting footpath, towards Newhaven and Charon Recycling.

★  ★  ★

Eden had not thought of what she would do when she arrived. She had no plan, other than the need to warn Billy. Did she really think his life was in danger?

Absolutely.

Whenever Eden thought of her meeting with Max Charon and his son Jagger, she always pictured that shark swimming past the window. The three of them were interchangeable in her mind, all of them predators.

At least the shark knew no better. Max and Jagger had no such excuse.

Eden made good time on the footpath and ran through the town, past Surf It! and down towards the massive recycling plant.

*Or weapons manufacturer, depending on your point of view*, Eden thought.

The wind had transformed into a

howling gale sending holidaymakers and shoppers indoors. The sky was growing darker as the storm clouds approached, and the sea looked as if it was boiling, it was so choppy and rough.

As Eden approached the gated entrance of Charon Recycling, her stomach contracted. An ambulance waited outside, lights flashing silently.

Eden picked up speed once more. She drew level with the ambulance, with the paramedics shutting the back doors.

'What's happened?' she gasped.

'Nasty accident,' the female paramedic said, and turned to walk away. The wind had snatched her words away, and Eden wasn't sure she had heard properly.

Eden scooted around in front of her.

'Is it Billy? Is Billy in there?'

The paramedic had looked as if she was about to lose her temper with Eden, but her face softened at the mention of Billy's name.

'Are you family?' she asked.

'I'm a friend — a close friend,' Eden replied.

The paramedic hesitated a moment. Eden said, 'He's dead, isn't he?'

The paramedic placed a hand on Eden's arm. 'No, he's alive, but he's in a bad way. We need to go, get him the help he needs in hospital.'

Eden stood and watched helplessly as the ambulance drove away. The siren burst briefly into life as it approached a junction.

Eden burst into tears.

*　*　*

'It's not your fault,' Jim said, handing Eden a cup of tea. 'You can't blame yourself.'

'Yes, I can, and I do,' Eden said, gripping the hot cup between her hands. 'Billy said he was in danger and I ignored him.'

Jim sat down next to Eden and placed a comforting hand on her shoulder. Eden, not knowing what else to do, had rushed straight over to Surf It!, hoping that Jim would be there to give comfort and perhaps help her decide what to do next.

'You couldn't have known this would happen. We don't even know *what* happened yet. This might have nothing at all to do with this Billy fellow coming to see you yesterday.'

'It's a bit of a coincidence though, isn't it?'

'Yes,' Jim said, speaking a little more firmly. 'And that's all it is, I'm sure about that.'

'And what about Finn? He's the only one who could have told Max Charon that lie about the lawyers helping Simeon. Don't you see, Finn has secretly been working for Max Charon all along!'

Jim sat and mulled this over for a few moments.

'And you're not sure that he can even surf?'

Eden shook her head. She was still clutching the hot cup of tea between her hands. The pain wasn't really registering in her brain.

Jim got up and walked over to his

computer. He sat down and began typing.

'If he's entered any events in the last year, or if he's a member of any surfing communities online, we should be able to find him.'

Eden stared into the cup of tea. Too milky and weak, as usual. Jim had never been able to make a decent tea or coffee as long as she had known him. And yet today, that was a comfort to her. Something stable and solid in her life.

'Nothing,' Jim said, finally. 'I'm sorry.'

'You think I'm right now, don't you?' Eden said, glumly.

'I don't know, but it's starting to look that way.'

A knock at the shop door startled them both.

'I'm . . . ah . . . sorry to disturb you,' Tom Maddox said, walking inside and fighting against the wind to close the door. He looked just as dishevelled as yesterday. More so, in fact.

'Can I help you?' Jim said, standing up.

Maddox held out his hand. 'Tom Maddox, reporter for the South Cornwall Gazette.'

Jim shook hands with him. 'Oh yes, Eden mentioned you.'

Maddox tilted his head back so that he could peer down his glasses, perched almost on the tip of his nose, at Eden. 'Have you, um, have you heard the news?'

'About Billy?' Eden said.

Maddox nodded and slid his glasses up onto the bridge of his nose. They immediately slid down again.

'Yes, yes, about Billy,' he agreed sombrely.

Eden nodded. A tear landed in her tea.

'So what happened, do you know?' Jim said.

'He was hit by a forklift truck that was reversing,' Maddox said. 'Apparently he had strayed into a loading bay where he had no business being. No one knows why he was there, without the proper permission and not wearing any safety gear.'

'That's horrible,' Eden said.

'Of course, we know it wasn't an accident, don't we?' Maddox said.

Jim raised an eyebrow. 'Is that what the police are saying? They're treating it as suspicious?'

'Well, um, no they're not,' Maddox replied. 'Not yet, at least. But they will.'

'It's obvious, isn't it?' Eden said. 'Finn was there when Billy told us what Charon Labs are up to, and reported back to his uncle. They had to get rid of Billy before he gathered any proof.'

'I don't know,' Jim replied. 'We seem to be jumping to a lot of conclusions here.'

'But it all happened so fast!' Eden said. 'It was only this morning that Billy came to see us.'

Maddox glanced around the workshop as though looking for hidden eavesdroppers. 'They have spies everywhere. You should be careful.'

'You know they're making guns?' Eden said.

'Guns,' Maddox repeated, as though he was trying the word out for the very first time. 'Ah, um, yes, I suppose I did.'

'You suppose?' Jim said. Before he could ask any more, his mobile began vibrating where it lay on his desk.

He picked it up. 'Hello?' Pause. 'Don't worry, she's here.' Another pause while he listened. 'All right, see you soon.'

'Was that Finn?'

'No, it was Larry. They're worried about you.'

'What about Finn?'

'They haven't seen him,' Jim replied.

'He's probably scuttled back to his uncle, now he knows you're onto him,' Maddox said.

'But they're coming down here to meet us,' Jim said, ignoring Maddox's comment. 'Doug's got something to tell us, apparently.'

'What are we going to do, Jim?' Eden wailed. 'I can't believe this is all happening!'

Jim crouched down beside Eden and

placed a fatherly arm around her shoulders.

'Don't worry, none of this is your fault and we can sort it out.' He looked up at Maddox. 'So? Are you taking what you know to the police?'

'Yes, of course,' Maddox said. 'I'm going to do that now, and report back to the office.'

Jim watched him leave. He waited until the door had been shut, and said, 'You know, there's something about that man that I do not like. Not one bit.'

# 12

Finn stood in the reception area of Charon Recycling, his hands stuffed in the pockets of his baggy shorts, and tried not to stare at the security guard. Was it just his imagination, or had security been beefed up since his last visit?

He stabbed a finger at the lift's call button again, impatient for it to arrive. When he had first turned up, demanding to see his uncle, reception had made a call to Charon and then told Finn that someone would be straight up to see him. But the minutes had dragged by, and still there was no sign of his uncle, or Jagger.

Beside the lift were the doors to the stairs, but he'd already found the doors were locked, and the only way of unlocking them was with a pass.

So Finn was left standing at the lift, waiting for Jagger or Uncle Max to come and get him.

Of course this whole delay was nothing more than a tactic to unsettle Finn, to put him on the back foot. He knew how they worked. Power and getting the upper hand was what mattered to the Charons.

If only they knew though, that Finn didn't need unsettling any more than he already was. Seeing Eden flinch from his touch, from his very presence, had been bad enough. But then watching as she leapt from her room window, slide down the drainpipe and run away rather than stay and talk to him had been even worse.

Since the moment they met, Eden had run hot and cold with Finn — but even for her, jumping out of a first-floor window seemed extreme. It was as if she was actually scared of him.

Finally, the lift doors swooshed open and Jagger stepped out, looking sharp as usual in his fitted shirt and trousers, and pointed shoes.

'Finn!' he said, stepping up close to

his cousin, getting right into his personal space. 'We've seen more of you in the last couple of days than we have in the last five years. Are you trying to weasel your way back into the family business?'

Finn decided the best tactic was to play by their rules, and stepped up even closer to Jagger so that they were face to face, only inches apart.

'What's going on, Jagger?'

Jagger raised his eyebrows.

'You're going to have to enlighten me a little Finn, I'm not a mind reader.'

'Is it true what I've heard? You're making weapons out of recycled plastic?'

'Ooh, I say, you have got your knickers in a twist, haven't you?' Jagger said, smiling.

'This isn't funny,' Finn hissed. 'Where's Uncle Max? He'll tell me what's going on.'

Jagger smirked. 'He's expecting you.'

Neither spoke as the lift made its swift descent underground. Finn's stomach was a knot of tension. All of a sudden he had the feeling that he was out of his depth here, that there were things going on he didn't understand.

Again his thoughts turned back to Eden. Why was she suddenly so scared of him? Finn had a feeling that he might find the answers he needed back here, at Charon Recycling. But he wasn't so sure they would be answers he wanted to hear.

Once they were out of the lift, Jagger led Finn to Max's office.

The old man was sitting at his desk in front of the picture window looking out onto the glorified aquarium. There was no sign of the shark.

Charon had been making an origami model, but when he saw Finn he scooped the paper and the scissors back into his drawer and stood up.

'Finn! How lovely to see you again so soon.'

He walked around his desk, arms held out in greeting.

Finn ignored the invitation to embrace.

'What's going on, Uncle Max? Is what I hear true? Are you a weapons manufacturer now?'

Charon sighed and shook his head sadly.

'Why do you always have such a low opinion of me, Finn? Your father and I made a promise, that one of us would look after both of you boys if the other passed away unexpectedly, and that is what I have tried to do with you. But you just won't let me.'

Finn balled his hands into fists. 'No, because you're corrupt, and you always have been.'

Charon held out his hands in a placatory gesture. 'I'm so sorry you think that way, Finn. Here I am trying to do my best, trying to be eco-friendly and help the planet by recycling, but this is the thanks I get. My only nephew accuses me of corruption.'

'Then answer the question, Uncle Max,' Finn snarled. 'Are you a weapons manufacturer now?'

'Tell him, Dad,' Jagger said. 'Tell him

216

what he wants to know.'

Max Charon sighed. Finn couldn't believe it, but he almost felt sorry for the old man at that moment. But what he had to say next changed all that.

'Yes, Finn, I am,' Charon said softly.

Finn took a deep breath. This was it, then. He had always known his family were unscrupulous in their business dealings, but turning to weapons manufacture? That was a whole new level of low.

'You're horrified, as I knew you would be,' Charon said.

'Hasn't got the stomach for the real world, more like,' Jagger sneered. 'He would rather hang out with his drippy hippy friends, and like, be cool, man.'

'Jagger, be quiet,' Charon said.

Jagger looked as if he had been slapped.

'Come with us, come and look at what we do,' Charon said to Finn.

A subdued Jagger walked over to the boardroom's double doors and opened them. Max Charon joined him. They turned to look at Finn, who hadn't moved.

'What's wrong, Finn?' Charon said. 'This is what you wanted, isn't it? To find out the truth? All of it?'

'I suppose so,' Finn said, suddenly unsure if he did want to know after all.

Jagger led the way out of the boardroom. Finn glanced back and caught a flash of grey as the great white shark cruised by, illuminated by spotlights in the water.

Out of the boardroom they turned right, away from the lift and the stairs. Finn noticed there was no door at the bottom of the stairs.

Through another door, and suddenly they were stepping into a huge, industrial warehouse. The noise of the machinery reverberated through the concrete floor. To their right, Finn saw the ramp leading up to the parking area at the front of Charon Recycling. A forklift truck was making its way down, carrying a huge, rusty skip.

'This is where the waste plastic

arrives and is sorted into the different types,' Charon said, having to speak up to make himself heard.

The fork lift truck reached the bottom of the ramp. Its skip was overflowing with plastic items: empty milk cartons, fruit punnets, cleaning bottles, clear plastic wrap, all the detritus of modern living. The truck drove over to a large, ugly-looking machine and began emptying its load onto a conveyor belt.

The plastic waste was delivered into the machine's open mouth by the conveyor belt.

'This machine automatically sorts out different types of plastic using a laser beam to measure thickness and density,' Charon continued. 'Once sorted, it can go to be shredded.'

They walked through the unit and into a second space, where a huge machine was shredding the sorted plastic into pellets and spitting them into containers.

'This is the stuff that's polluting the sea right now!' Finn yelled.

Charon nodded. 'Unfortunately, yes. When that old man's fishing boat scraped against the outside of our container of pellets waiting to be melted down, his anchor pulled a siding off, releasing the pellets out into the ocean.'

'You're still blaming that on Simeon?' Finn caught the look that passed between the old man and his son. 'Is this revenge?' Finn demanded of Jagger. 'Are you still annoyed about your brand new car getting dented?'

'It was more than a dent!' Jagger hissed. 'That old fool attacked my car with a wrench!'

'I know, I was there, remember?' Finn said. 'Best entertainment I've had all week.'

'All right you two, calm down,' Charon said. 'Let's continue the tour. It's not often I get to show people around.'

They moved on, into a third area. Here a long metal chute rattled as the shredded plastic flew down it and into another large, metallic contraption. Pipes of varying thickness crawled over the outer hub, and there was a panel on the side with various dials and controls. It looked strangely old-fashioned.

'This is where the pellets of plastic are melted,' Charon said. 'Each type of plastic has a different melting point and varying rigidity and strength when cooled back down. That's why they need sorting before they get shredded.'

'And what happens then?' Finn asked.

'The appropriate plastic, now in liquid form, is fed next door to our 3D printers,' Charon replied.

'And then what?' Finn said.

'I'll show you,' Charon said.

Charon led Finn into another part of the complex he hadn't seen before. They were in a large room, empty apart from a long, squat machine which looked like a glorified photocopier. Several touch screens adorned its sides and there was a glass casing at one end.

The machine was silent, the touch screens dark. Charon picked an object out of the glass casing and handed it to Finn.

The plastic gun looked like a toy, and it was incredibly light in Finn's hand.

'This is what you're making?' Finn said.

'One of many variations, yes,' Charon said.

'Don't be fooled by its looks,' Jagger said. 'It's lethal.'

'And undetectable at airports,' Charon said. 'This is the future of weapons manufacture, Finn. Low cost, using recycled materials, fast and efficient, and highly profitable.'

'You forgot about highly illegal and totally immoral,' Finn said, handing the gun to Jagger. The feel of its plastic casing in his hand had made his skin crawl.

'I suppose that depends on your point of view,' Charon said. 'One man's terrorist is another man's freedom fighter.'

'Which makes you worse than everyone, because you're just interested in selling to the highest bidder.'

'Join us, Finn,' Charon said, his face

suddenly eager, his voice pleading almost. 'Come back and join us in the family business. Your father would be proud of you, if he was still here. He would want you to be a part of this.'

'Don't waste your breath, Dad,' Jagger sneered. 'Look at him, such a do-gooder, he won't have anything to do with this.'

'He's right,' Finn said. 'I think it's time I left.'

Jagger and Charon made no move. The air was thick with tension.

'Where will you go, Finn?' Charon said softly. 'You can't go back to your new friends, you know,'

'Why not?' Finn said, but it seemed as though a switch had been flicked inside his head, opening a door to a realisation that he had been duped.

'Your friends believe you're a traitor, that you've secretly been working with your dear Uncle Max and cousin Jagger, that you infiltrated their friendship because we knew what a threat they were to our business. You're the one who told us about Billy, and you're the one who told us about Simeon's lawyers.'

'But none of that is true!' Finn snapped.

'We know that,' Jagger snarled, 'but your friends have a very different opinion of you now, including your pretty little girlfriend.'

'Leave Eden out of this!' Finn said.

'Oh, but we can't,' Charon said, smiling. 'Because she has been the one feeding us with information.'

'The reporter she talked about,' Finn said, as a cold, lead weight settled in his stomach. 'He's working with you, isn't he?'

Jagger started giggling. 'I told you it would work, Dad. Tom Maddox isn't even a reporter, he works for us!'

Charon was smiling as he looked at Finn.

'I thought you would all see right through his act. One call to the South Cornwall Gazette and his cover would have been blown. But no, Jagger was right, you are all so wrapped up in yourselves none of you even thought about doing a basic check on Maddox's credentials.'

Finn ground his teeth. He had been stupid, they all had. But he took most of the blame. He should have remembered how duplicitous his family was. Like snakes, they could slither in and out of any situation and loved causing mayhem and pain and misery.

'Come back to us, Finn,' Charon said, holding out a hand in invitation. 'Come back to your family, where you belong.'

Finn shook his head. 'No. Never.'

He made to leave, but Jagger stepped in front of him, blocking his way out.

'Not so fast, cuz,' he said.

'Get out of my way, Jagger,' Finn said, through gritted teeth.

'You think we're going to let you leave, after everything you've seen?' Jagger snarled.

'What are you going to do, keep me here as a prisoner?'

'Won't you change your mind?' Charon said.

Finn shook his head, but kept staring at Jagger.

'Then yes, I'm afraid we will have to keep you here as our prisoner, for the time being at least,' Charon said, a note of sadness in his voice.

'This is ridiculous,' Finn said, and stepped to one side, intending to stride past Jagger.

Jagger grabbed Finn by the arm and twisted it around and behind Finn's back.

Finn spun the other way and kicked Jagger's feet out from beneath him. Jagger let go as he fell on his back with a loud gasp of pain.

'I'm leaving,' Finn said, staring at Jagger on the floor. 'Now.'

'No, I'm afraid you're not,' Charon said. He had the printed plastic gun in his hand, and he was pointing it at Finn. 'I know it might look like a toy, but I promise you it's not. If you want to find out how lethal one of these firearms is, you can try and leave. But I suggest you don't.'

Finn stared at the gun as Jagger scrambled back to his feet.

'What are we going to do with him, Dad?' Jagger said.

'Take him back to the boardroom. Tie him to a chair while we think about it,' Charon replied.

'What is there to think about?' Jagger replied, his voice like ice. 'Doesn't matter how long we hold on to him for, as soon as we let him go he'll tell the police everything. We should just — '

'Take him to the boardroom!' Charon snapped. 'Leave the decision-making to me.'

Jagger grabbed Finn by the arm, his fingers squeezing tighter than they needed to.

Finn allowed himself to be led away.

He knew he had to come up with an escape plan, and quick. His Uncle Max might not be too keen to contemplate the idea just yet, but really there was only one thing they could do with Finn.

Murder him.

# 13

Doug could barely contain himself with excitement, but when he saw how upset Eden was the excitement quickly faded away.

Larry, Nina, Doug and Ellie crowded around her, concerned for her, wanting to help or give her comfort. They shot questions at her, placed hands on her shoulders and arms, and generally began to suffocate her.

Finally she had to tell them to back up before she drowned in their concern.

'Tell you what,' Jim said. 'As I already know that my tea and coffee making abilities are considered to be on a par with Genghis Khan's peacemaking skills, why don't I take us all out for a drink and a bite to eat?'

'Oh, I'm really not sure I could manage to — '

Larry cut Eden off. 'That sounds like a great idea. And then Doug can tell you guys his new info, and maybe we can work out what it means.'

Eden looked at Larry, her curiosity piqued.

'What are you talking about?'

'Uh-uh,' Larry said, waving a finger at her. 'Let's go get that drink and food first.'

They decamped to the Wave cafe. Jim ordered teas and coffees, along with paninis, wraps and baguettes. Eden hadn't thought she would be hungry, but when presented with her food, she realised she was ravenous and tucked in.

Brightened a little by the food and drink, she turned to Doug.

'So come on then, spill. What's this exciting information that we need to puzzle over?'

Doug pulled a sheaf of folded papers from the back pocket of his shorts and handed them to Eden.

'Billy messaged me on Facebook just

229

before his accident. He didn't say anything, just sent me a file. I printed it off at the hostel. Take a look.'

Eden pushed away her empty plate and unfolded the paper on the table. Jim, sitting next to her, leaned in to examine them.

Eden leafed through the papers, passing them to Jim. 'I don't understand. They're receipts, aren't they? For building materials.'

'Concrete, girders, glass, insulation,' Jim said as he leafed through the papers. 'All in massive quantities. I'd say these are the receipts for the building materials for the recycling plant. And look at the dates — all from four years back when the facility was first built.'

Eden looked up from studying the papers.

'So what does it mean?'

'Beats me,' said Doug. 'We were hoping you might have an idea, or maybe that reporter friend of yours.'

'I wouldn't say he's a friend,' Eden replied. 'But yes, I suppose it might be worth showing these to him.'

'They must be important, otherwise why would Billy have sent them to us?' Larry said, scooping up the last of his salad.

'Wasn't he supposed to be digging up proof of Charon's involvement in weapons manufacturing?' Jim said. 'All you've got here is a list of building materials used in the construction of the lab. There is not one item on this list that I can see that is suspicious.'

Eden sighed and rubbed her hands over her face. All of a sudden she was consumed by the need to get away from everyone, to grab her new board and launch herself into the sea. Not that that was going to happen with the storm brewing.

'Will you be in touch with that reporter anytime soon?' Nina said.

'I don't know,' Eden replied.

'Why not give him a call?'

'I haven't got his number,' Eden said.

'You forget,' Larry said, chuckling, 'Eden is old school and doesn't use this modern technology called the mobile phone.' He held up his index fingers and crossed them over each other. 'Sorcery! Black magic!'

Eden laughed along with the others.

'That's right, make fun of me, but you won't change my mind.'

'I don't get it,' Doug said. 'How do you keep up with your friends without access to Facebook?'

'I'm not even on Facebook,' Eden said.

Doug looked at her as though he couldn't actually comprehend what she had just said.

'What about Twitter, Instagram?'

Eden shook her head, grinning.

'Surely you can see the benefit in having WhatsApp? Or text messaging at least?'

Eden shook her head again. 'No, I hate it all. As long as I don't have a mobile I can disappear wherever I want and not have to worry about anybody else. And that's how I prefer it.'

'What is this strange creature?' Doug

said, turning to Larry. 'Is she from another planet?'

Jim pulled his mobile from his pocket. 'Let's call the South Cornwall Gazette. If he's not in the office, they should be able to give us his number.'

'Good idea,' Larry said, standing up. 'I for one need another drink. Anyone else? Coffee? Tea?'

Larry took orders while Jim looked up the number for the Gazette. Eden looked around the table at all her friends and was overcome with a rush of gratitude. There would be plenty of times from this point on where she travelled alone, but she knew she would never be lonely. Not as long as she had friends like these guys to watch her back, wherever in the world they might be.

'Hello, could I speak to Tom Maddox, please?' Jim said into his mobile as he turned away for a little privacy.

Ellie took hold of Eden's hand.

'I'm sorry about Finn — he seemed

such a nice guy. You two were perfect together.'

Nina took her other hand.

Eden smiled at them both, grateful for their friendship. 'Thank you.'

Doug, who had gone to help Larry with the drinks, returned with a coffee in each hand and placed them on the table.

Jim was still talking on the phone.

Larry returned with the rest of the drinks.

Jim turned back to face the others and placed his mobile on the table. His face was grim.

'What's wrong?' Eden said.

'The South Cornwall Gazette has no one on staff named Tom Maddox,' Jim said.

'Did you get the name of the newspaper right?' Doug said, looking at Eden.

She nodded. She could barely speak.

'The woman I spoke to at the Gazette was very helpful,' Jim said. 'She told me that she knew of no reporters in the area by that name. She even asked a couple of the other reporters while I was on the phone. Neither of them recognised the name Tom Maddox.'

No one spoke. The silence grew heavier, as they all turned this fresh news over in their minds.

'Do you think — ?' Larry said.

Eden cut him off. 'I've been tricked. That's what has happened.'

'Oh man,' Doug said, running his hands through his shaggy hair. 'You think this Maddox guy is working for Charon?'

'No, I don't *think* that,' Eden said. 'I *know* it.'

They all looked at Eden.

'Think about it,' she said. 'Maddox fed me the lie about Simeon getting lawyers to fight his case, so that we could see if Finn told it to his uncle. Then Maddox phoned me back the next day to tell me that's what had happened. He lied to me. He took a gamble, that I would carry through the plan we had cooked up together, or that I had thought we cooked up together, and that I would tell Finn the lie that Maddox invented. There is no mole at Charon Labs, and Finn didn't betray us.'

'What about Billy?' Larry said.

Eden's hands flew to her mouth.

'That was my fault. I told Maddox about Billy, and so he told Charon!'

Jim placed a hand gently on Eden's shoulder.

'It's not your fault, you didn't know.'

'But it is my fault,' Eden said. 'And I'm going to put it right. Maddox and Charon need to pay for what they did.'

'We should go to the police,' Larry said.

'But what proof do we have?' Nina said. 'We have nothing, just a suspicion that Billy's accident wasn't an accident at all.'

'What about Simeon?' Larry said.

'What about him?' Eden said. 'Charon Labs are within their rights to bring a prosecution against him for trespassing.'

Larry sighed and threw his hands in the air.

'All right, all right, so what do we do next?'

Jim tapped the pile of papers on the table. 'This must mean something, or why would Billy have sent it to us? I have a friend who's a building contractor. Why don't I let him have a look? Maybe he can spot something we're missing.'

'Good idea,' Eden said. 'And I'm going back to the hostel to tell Finn what's going on. He must be very confused right now — the last time he saw me I was leaping out of my window and sliding down a drainpipe!'

'Great, let's reconvene later this evening, shall we?' Doug said.

★   ★   ★

Eden sat at the kitchen table in the hostel, watching the trees blowing in the gale, the distant sea churned up by the elements. All afternoon she had been waiting for Finn, but there was no sign of him, or his camper van. At first, Eden had begun to worry that maybe

Finn had left, packed up and gone somewhere, anywhere, to get away from this situation with his family.

Eden worried that he must be feeling incredibly lonely. His Uncle Max and his cousin were villains, and now it must seem to him that Eden wanted nothing to do with him.

Eden hated the thought that she might have driven him away, and she was scared that she might never see him again. Eventually she talked to Martin, who confirmed that Finn had not checked out.

Her relief was tempered with confusion and concern. Where on earth was he?

Eden spent the rest of the afternoon at the kitchen table, keeping watch for Selina the camper van to come rolling into the car park, black smoke belching from the exhaust pipe. As soon as she saw Finn she intended to run outside to him, throw her arms around him and explain everything.

And maybe she would never let go.

But by evening Finn still hadn't returned and she was growing worried. Something had happened to him, she was sure. And that something probably involved his uncle and cousin.

Her friends returned — Larry and Nina first, followed by Doug and Ellie with Jim in tow. They stood in the hostel entrance brushing rainwater off their clothes and out of their hair. In the few seconds it had taken them to run from their cars, they had been drenched by the downpour.

Despite this, Jim was very excited.

Nina filled the kettle and made drinks. They sat at the table, and Jim produced the papers Doug had given him.

'I talked to my friend about these supply receipts, and we think we know what they mean,' he said.

'Well, don't keep us in suspense, this isn't *Who Wants To Be A Millionaire?*,' Eden said.

'He's been like this the entire way back,' Larry said. 'Refused to tell us a thing until we got back here.'

'Derek pulled up the plans for Charon Labs on the internet,' Jim said. 'Apparently they are available to view by anyone, as there was some Lottery money pumped into the project as well as private financing. Derek compared the architectural drawings to the supply receipts. It took him a while, but he found a discrepancy.'

Jim stared at everyone, hardly able to keep a triumphant grin off his face.

'Jim, are you going to tell us or do we have to tickle it out of you?' Nina said.

'The supplies of concrete, lengths of reinforced beams and girders, the amount of glass, the electrical cabling, everything really, there's far too much of it. It seems they were building something much bigger than the facility they ended up with.'

'That's crazy,' Ellie said. 'It doesn't make sense at all.'

'Yes, it does,' Eden said. 'There's a whole section of Charon Labs that nobody knows about. That's where they will be printing weapons.'

'And all the time the so-called honest side of the business carries on in the public-facing part of the building,' Jim said. 'It's very clever.'

'But how does this knowledge help us?' Larry said. 'Do you think the police would take any notice if we turned up with a list of building supplies as proof of something dodgy going on?'

'No,' Eden said. 'And we've got another problem, I'm afraid, guys. I haven't seen Finn since this morning. Has anyone else seen him today?'

No one else had, either.

'I don't like it,' Eden said. 'Something's happened to him — I know it has.'

# 14

After a restless night, Eden woke anxious and tired. Her fears for Finn's safety had kept her from sleeping properly, but the noise of the wind howling around the youth hostel, and the rain hammering at the windows, hadn't helped.

The storm that had been predicted for days was definitely here. It fitted Eden's mood perfectly.

She padded downstairs on her bare feet and sat alone in the kitchen, gazing out at the rain, lashing at the cars parked outside, and the window just inches from her face. Another day loomed with no opportunity to surf. The prospect of the hours stretching ahead, with nothing to do but worry about Finn while feeling helpless, depressed her terribly.

'Good morning.' Doug entered the kitchen.

'Hey,' Eden said, turning away from

the depressing sight of the rain.

'How did you sleep?'

'Never better,' Eden said, with a rueful smile.

Doug laughed. 'Me too.'

'Do you think this rain will stop anytime soon?' Eden said, turning back to look out of the window.

'According to the news, it's going to get worse before it gets better,' Doug said. 'The beach clean-up has been abandoned until tomorrow at the earliest.'

'That's a shame,' Eden said.

'The worry is that the powerful winds and rough sea are going to disperse that shredded plastic making it even more difficult to collect.'

'And so poisoning the marine ecosystem even more,' Eden concluded for him.

'That's right.' Doug paused. 'No word from Finn, I'm guessing?'

Eden shook her head. 'I tried calling the police earlier, but we're not allowed to report him missing until this evening at the earliest. Even then I doubt they will do much other than get us to fill out a couple of forms.'

'There's got to be something we can do,' Doug said, joining Eden by the window, and putting a comforting arm over her shoulders. 'Maybe we should pay Charon Recycling a visit, ask them what they know.'

Eden shook her head. 'They won't talk to us.'

'I suppose not,' Doug said.

Eden took a deep breath. 'I can't just hang around here all day, though. I'm going to pay Billy a visit in hospital. If he's able to talk, he might be able to give me some new information. Besides, I feel I owe him a visit. It's the least I can do.'

Doug gave her a gentle squeeze.

'Just remember, none of this is your fault. This is all down to Max and Jagger Charon, yeah?'

Eden nodded, but she couldn't shrug off the heavy feeling of guilt.

★ ★ ★

Eden sat in the hard hospital chair by Billy's bed. The ward was clean and quiet, the walls an antiseptic white. A large machine beeped softly, a wire leading from it to Billy's hand where a clip had been attached to his index finger.

Billy was asleep, and the nurse had said Eden could sit with him but not disturb him. His face was badly bruised and swollen, and the parts of his torso and arms not covered with the sheet had been wrapped in bandages. His left arm was in a long cast, from his wrist to his shoulder.

As she sat there, a tear rolled down her cheek. The guilt was heavy on her shoulders. She had told Maddox about Billy, who had told Max Charon. It was her fault that Billy was lying here, broken so badly the nurse had said his injuries were life changing.

There was nothing Eden could do for Billy. But she could sit here, even if only for a little while. She promised herself she would come back every day, do what she could to help his recovery.

Eden didn't know if he had family or friends — he had seemed a lonely kind of person.

More pressing than her concern for Billy though was her fear for Finn's safety. No one knew for sure that he had gone to Charon Labs to confront his uncle and cousin, but what other explanation could there be? His belongings were still in his room and he hadn't checked out.

Finn was being held captive by Max and Jagger. It was the only explanation.

Larry had decided to call the police again. Eden and the others sat and listened to his side of the conversation as he attempted to explain what had happened. Even to Eden's ears, Larry had sounded like a delusional conspiracy theorist.

'They said there's nothing they can do yet,' Larry had said when he'd finished the call. 'Apparently the Health and Safety Executive will be the first ones to investigate Billy's accident, and if they suspect something they then pass it on to the police. As for Finn, since he's been missing less than twenty-four hours at the moment, they won't classify him as a missing person.'

Twenty-four hours. Even then, Eden suspected the wheels of the investigation would grind slowly. By then it might be too late for Finn. Max Charon and Jagger had already proved themselves capable of extreme measures in their effort to silence Billy. Would they hesitate to do the same to Finn? Eden thought not.

But what could Eden do? Billy had been her only contact inside Charon Labs. There was no one else she could turn to for help.

She wiped at her eyes.

A nurse approached and smiled gently at Eden.

'I'm afraid I'll have to ask you to leave in a minute,' she said. 'The doctors will be round.'

Eden nodded. The nurse checked out a few readings on the machine's digital displays.

Billy murmured slightly, and the nurse leaned over him and checked his dressings. His bruised eyes flickered slightly, but didn't open. The lashes were thick with a green, crusted scum.

'Let's just give you a little clean,' the nurse said softly to Billy. She looked up at Eden. 'In the cabinet, there's a packet of facial wipes.'

Eden opened the cupboard just by her seat and saw the wipes straight away. She passed the packet to the nurse who pulled out a wipe and began gently cleaning Billy's face, around his mouth and his nose and his eyes.

Looking at the cupboard as she was about to close the door, Eden noticed a small pile of Billy's belongings. A couple of pens, his wallet, some loose change . . . and an ID pass on a lanyard.

Eden glanced at the nurse. She was preoccupied with caring for Billy.

Not thinking about what she was doing, Eden took the ID pass and shoved it into her pocket.

'I should go now,' she said, standing up.

The stolen pass felt hot in her pocket, as if it was going to burn its way through the fabric and drop to the floor, accusing her of theft.

The nurse smiled. 'You can come back tomorrow. We'll look after him.'

Eden hurried out of the ward and out of the hospital. She couldn't quite believe what she had just done. It had been a spur-of-the-moment decision — not even a decision really but instinct. And she had to ask herself, what did she think she could achieve by stealing Billy's ID pass for Charon Recycling?

She could get inside. And rescue Finn.

\* \* \*

'Are you mad?' Larry said, when Eden had explained her plan. 'So, you're going to simply walk up to the front door and let yourself in? And then have a wander around, looking for Finn?'

'Well, when you put it like that . . . '
Eden said.

'It sounds mad, which it is,' Larry
finished for her. 'There's no way it will
work.'

Eden's spirits sank. She'd been
hoping she could convince Larry and
the others to help her, but now that
didn't look likely.

'The problem is,' Doug said, 'you
can't just turn up at the front door and
wave Billy's pass at them. Sure, this will
probably get you through the gates without the need for buzzing the intercom,
but once inside, you have to justify why
you're there. And I imagine security is
pretty tight.'

'And you're already a known face
there,' Larry said. 'You'll be recognised
right away.'

'Maybe she could go in disguise,'
Nina said.

'What, like Tom Cruise in *Mission
Impossible*?' Doug said.

Larry slapped the palm of his hand

on the table. 'Man, I knew I should have brought my wigs and facial prosthetic kit with me!'

Nina punched him on the shoulder. 'Hey, I'm only trying to help! Have you got a better idea?'

'The problem is, even if you did get past security, you don't know how many doors this will open,' Larry said, picking up the pass.

'I don't need it to open any doors,' Eden said. 'There's a lift, and it only has two buttons on it, one for the ground floor and another for the first. But I've seen Jagger swiping his security pass at the panel, and the lift goes down, underground.'

'And you think Billy has the same permission on his pass?' Doug said.

'Wouldn't he?'

Larry shook his head. 'Not necessarily. Billy would probably only have security clearance up to a certain level, and I doubt he was cleared to go anywhere they might be holding Finn.'

Eden's spirits sank even lower. 'So

you're saying there's no point even trying?'

Larry and Doug looked at each other, and their faces split into wide grins.

'No way,' Doug said. 'I mean hey, let's not fool ourselves, any attempt to get in to Charon Recycling is probably doomed to failure, but let's do it anyway.'

'Absolutely,' Larry replied, and took Eden's hand in his. 'After all, where would the fun be if we already knew it was going to work?'

# 15

The plastic waste undulated on the surface of the sea, its swell powerful and frightening. It was unnerving, like looking at a mountain of rubbish that had come to life, or like sitting on the back of a massive, multi-coloured dragon as it flew through the sky.

Nina was sitting in the front of the dinghy, digging her paddle into the water and thrusting powerfully back. Eden, sitting behind her and with a rucksack strapped to her back, matched Nina's powerful strokes with her own. They pushed their way through the mass of plastic like a ship ploughing through ice in the Arctic.

The rain pounded them with a frightening intensity. The sea lifted them high and then dropped them again in its powerful swell, over and over. Eden was grateful she had never suffered from seasickness — although she was thinking that much more of this and there might well be a first time.

They were officially trespassing now, in the area that Max Charon claimed Simeon had been. A featureless wall stretched up ahead of them, the waves crashing against it. This was the side of Charon's Labs that could only be seen from the sea, and it looked even uglier than the front-facing section, which Eden hadn't thought possible.

The two women kept up their rhythm, paddling alongside the blank wall of concrete and steel, careful not to get too close where they would be thrown against it by the powerful waves. Eden imagined the wall as it disappeared below the water line. She wondered if down there was where Max Charon's glorified aquarium was located, where the great white shark lived. She imagined it escaping somehow, shooting up to the surface and snatching Eden in its jaws, pulling her back down below the surface.

'There,' Nina shouted, pointing to a

spot beyond the featureless wall at the rocky cliff face.

'I see it,' Eden yelled back.

There was a gap in the rock face, a dark cave. The two women dug deeper with their paddles, anxious to get this part over with. Navigating their way inside the cave without being dashed against the rocks was going to be the most difficult and dangerous part of the whole exercise.

Well — until Eden smuggled herself inside Charon Recycling. Then the dangerous part really would begin.

Nina pointed back out to sea, indicating that they were too close to the cliff face. The two women worked hard at turning the dinghy around. Eden's shoulders ached from the effort, and what seemed like a never-ending struggle to force the dinghy through the sea and keep it in the direction they needed to go.

If a member of the lifeguard service happened to see them out on the water in these conditions, there would be hell to pay when, or if, they got back on land. But Eden was desperate, and this was their only chance.

Once they had the dinghy far enough away from the rocks to avoid being dashed against them, the two women worked at turning it back around to face the cave. Thankfully the dark gap in the rocks was wide; in calm conditions there would be no trouble in navigating the dinghy inside.

But these were far from calm conditions, and Eden knew they had their work cut out for them to keep from being bashed against the sharp rocks.

Without needing to discuss what they were doing, both Eden and Nina dug their paddles deep into the water. They had to keep up a powerful rhythm, try and force themselves down an imaginary line right through the middle of the hole in the rock face. But it was hard, with the ocean tossing them up and down and the rain pounding their heads, water running down their faces and into their eyes.

They were on the crest of a huge swell, the cave visible and directly ahead of them, when the ocean suddenly seemed to disappear beneath the dinghy. They dropped with a sickening abruptness, and where a moment before there had been a view of the rocks in front of them and the horizon behind them there was now nothing but a wall of water surrounding them.

'Paddle!' Nina screamed.

Eden dug deep into her reserves of strength and energy. This constant battle with the ocean was exhausting her. She was used to cooperating with it, harnessing its power, not fighting it.

The wall of water grew taller and darker, towering over them, reducing Eden and Nina to two tiny figures in a frail looking dinghy.

Sea water crashed over them, and what felt like the entire ocean slammed into Eden's back and threw her onto the dinghy's floor. Spluttering and coughing, she held on tight, hauling herself upright. The dinghy was full of water and multi-coloured plastic pellets, but they weren't sinking, not yet. The ocean's swell was carrying them up again.

Fast.

Eden gripped the sides of the dinghy. She had lost her paddle, and she could see Nina had lost hers too. They were now at the mercy of the ocean.

The swell carried them up to its peak, where Eden could see the dark grey sky again and the cliff face charging towards them. Eden screwed her eyes shut as the fragile dinghy began descending once more. The ocean didn't want them any more; they were intruders and needed ejecting.

This was going to hurt.

The dinghy spun around as it was flung back and forth. To Eden it felt like a theme park ride, the most extreme, dangerous ride in the world. She gripped the nylon handles on the edge of the dinghy as hard as she could as powerful waves smashed into her and over her.

But they were being propelled forward. What Eden didn't know was, where they going to be thrown into the cave or dashed against the rocks?

All of a sudden the noise of the ocean changed, growing deeper and more echoing. And their momentum was fading, and fast. Eden opened her eyes. They were inside the cave — and the ocean's swell was weaker.

Nina jumped out of the dinghy and began hauling it onto a small, pebbled beach. Eden followed and helped her. They dragged the dinghy up the beach until it was out of reach of the waves pulling and sucking at the pebbles and smashing against the sides of the cave.

The two women collapsed on the tiny beach and started laughing.

'I thought we were going to die, for sure!' Eden gasped, wiping water off her face.

'It was a bit scary there for a moment, wasn't it?' Nina shouted over the sound of the waves crashing against the rocks.

'A bit?' Eden yelled. 'That's the

understatement of the year!'

Nina laughed. 'Well, we made it.'

They were both wearing head torches. Now they switched them on, climbed to their feet and walked deeper into the cave. Eden looked up, the beam from her head torch illuminating dark, rocky walls, dripping with moisture.

'Wow, this is amazing,' she said, her voice echoing off the walls.

'It's known locally as Cinders Hole,' Nina replied. 'Legend says that it was used by smugglers in the sixteenth century.'

'And there's a way up?' Eden said.

Nina pointed to a narrow channel carved into the side of the rock, formed over millennia by the force of the sea or the movement of the land.

'Up there, but you've got to climb. You're OK with climbing, aren't you?'

Eden grinned. 'Just watch me.'

She tightened her rucksack straps as she gazed up at the climb she was about to attempt.

'It forms a tunnel as you climb higher

and gets a bit of a tight squeeze, but you should be fine,' Nina said. 'Before Charon bought up this whole area and built his recycling plant, this tunnel leading down to Cinders Hole had a name — The Chimney.'

Eden looked up, trying to spot the opening.

'Don't go lighting a fire while I'm up there, will you?' she said.

'If I think you need to get a move on, maybe,' Nina replied.

Eden contemplated the Chimney a few moments longer. 'OK. See you later,' she said finally, and began climbing.

Her trainers had plenty of grip and were a good match for the sharp, angular edges of the rock face. She'd also brought gloves. Without them Eden was sure her hands would be bleeding by the time she reached the top.

Foothold by foothold, handhold by handhold, Eden inched her way up the natural chimney. Nina was right, the sides began closing in on her, the higher she climbed. At one point her foot slipped on the wet rock. Eden had to jam her back against the side, her rucksack cushioning her from the hard edges, while she recovered her nerve.

The fall would be a long, hard one, bouncing off the sharp edges and cutting her to ribbons.

After taking a moment to recover, Eden began climbing again. The rocky walls closed in even more. The rucksack became a hindrance, catching on the rock, holding her back. Her arms grew tired, having to constantly hold them above shoulder height. The tight space limited how much she could bend her knees and she had to work harder to find footholds.

But there was a light up above her. The faint grey of daylight, of the sun hidden behind storm clouds. Eden hauled herself up, her feet slipping on the jagged footholds more and more often. The space was so tight now, she wondered if she would fall even if she let go . . .

And then the panic set in. Her feet

were dangling in the space below her. She was even able to let go of the handholds. She was trapped. Jammed in place, with no one to help her get out. She would be stuck here until she starved to death . . .

'Don't be an idiot,' Eden grunted. 'Now pull yourself together and get out of here.'

Hardly able to bend her knees, Eden had to work hard to scramble into a position where her feet found purchase against the sides of the Chimney. They were no more than toe holds really, but they would have to do. Finding the best hand holds she could, Eden pulled and pushed, clenching her teeth as she grunted with the effort.

She managed to push herself up, but only by a couple of inches.

With both feet on new footholds, Eden stretched her arms upwards, straining for a handhold above her head. Her fingertips found one, scrabbling for purchase. She flicked bits of wet grit on her face, but by pushing with her feet she was able to get a better purchase and haul herself up again.

Thankfully the tunnel opened out slightly, giving a little more freedom of movement. The sound of the waves crashing into the cave had receded below her, and now she could hear the rain up above, and feel droplets of it on her face.

Eden concentrated on her breathing, on finding handholds and footholds. Everything else was a distraction. The tight squeeze of the Chimney, the storm, Max and Jagger Charon, Finn. All that mattered at the moment was climbing higher.

Almost before she realised what had happened, Eden found herself at the top. Bathed in a subdued, grey daylight, she tilted her head back . . . and found herself only inches from an iron grill, placed over the hole in the ground.

She placed her hands against the cold, rough iron and pushed.

The iron cover didn't move.

Eden's arms ached from the climb,

and the constant tension in her muscles. Now she was stuck, unable to climb any further.

What now? Climb back down? Surely she couldn't give up at this point, not when she was so close?

And there was no way she could see herself getting through that tight squeeze where the Chimney narrowed again.

Rainwater dripped on her face. The rain was as heavy as ever. Eden could hear the wind, and something crashing to the ground. If only the weather could have been a little kinder to them. The storm had only made their rescue mission more difficult.

But no one had said it would be easy in the first place. And having come this far, Eden wasn't about to give up now.

Jamming her feet into crevasses in the rock, she planted her hands against the cold grillwork and pushed with everything she had. The cover shifted slightly. Encouraged, Eden pushed harder.

Suddenly the cover lifted, tearing at

grass and soil and dislodging pebbles. Eden pushed until her exit was completely free, and hauled herself out of the natural rock chimney.

She lay on her side, panting, almost oblivious to the rain and the wind battering her, the water running off her face. There was no time to rest, though. She had to get a move on.

Climbing to her feet, Eden ran over to find a little shelter against the side of the Charon Recycling building. She pulled the rucksack off and opened the zipper. Charon Recycling towered above her, but again there were no windows in the blank façade. There was a lone security camera, but Eden couldn't do anything about that. She just had to hope no one was monitoring it right now.

Quickly she changed into the overalls she had brought with her and placed a cap on her head. The disguise was a pretty lame attempt at looking like a worker of some indeterminate kind, but it would have to do.

Eden pulled a mobile phone from the

rucksack. It was Larry's. Quickly she sent a text to Doug.

*I'm ready.*

Now to see if their half-baked plan might actually work.

* * *

'Where is he?' Doug yelled, spinning around on the spot. 'Come on out here, you coward!'

'Doug,' Ellie pleaded, 'please calm down.'

'Get off me!' Doug snarled, pushing Ellie away. 'You've done enough damage.'

Doug began stalking through the large reception area of Charon Labs, twisting his head this way and that.

'Where is he?' he yelled. 'Where's that lying cheat, Jagger?'

Two overweight security guards wobbled their way towards Doug, clutching at their belts, their keys jangling.

Ellie, for no apparent reason, tilted her head back and screamed. The two security guards paused, obviously unsure which problem they should deal with first. The man at the reception desk picked up a telephone and made a call, speaking urgently into the receiver.

'Sir, Madam, could you please both calm down?' one of the security guards said.

'Get me that snake Jagger Charon, and I'll show you how calm I can be once I've punched his lights out!' Doug yelled.

Ellie screamed again. Anyone who knew her would realise she was actually enjoying herself.

The lift doors swooshed open and Jagger Charon stepped out.

'What's going on?' he snapped, striding across the foyer towards Doug and Ellie.

Unnoticed by anyone apart from Ellie, who decided at that moment to let rip with another ear-piercing scream, Eden stepped into the elevator.

The doors closed.

★ ★ ★

Eden swiped Billy's pass across the blank plate fitted beneath the ground and first floor buttons. Nothing happened. She tried again, slower.

Still nothing.

Eden squeezed her eyes shut. Larry had been right, Billy never had access to the more private reaches of Charon Labs. Why would he?

It had been a desperate gamble, and Doug and Larry had been clear about their slim chances of success. But it had been their only hope, and at the very least they'd had to try.

Still, she was inside Charon Recycling and she would just have to find another way of getting to Finn. They couldn't stop her. Eden couldn't let them. There was too much at —

Eden opened her eyes.

The elevator had begun its swift descent.

*Billy's pass worked after all!* Eden thought.

Her insides tightened with fear at the thought of what she might find when the lift doors opened.

*What am I doing? What am I doing? What am I doing? Larry was right, I'm mad. I was bonkers to even think of this, let alone go ahead with it.*

The elevator pinged as it slowed down and came to a halt.

Eden took a deep breath. Crazy or not, she was here now. Time to find Finn, and then get them both out.

The lift doors slid open.

'Hello, Eden,' Tom Maddox said.

# 16

Eden walked silently beside Maddox as he led her down the underground corridor. Even down here, deep underground, Eden could hear the low rumble of the storm outside. She hoped Nina was all right, back in the cave.

'Aren't you, ah, going to ask me how I knew you were here?' Maddox said.

'Does it matter?' Eden replied. She genuinely did not care.

Maddox pushed his glasses back up onto the bridge of his nose. 'We saw you on the security camera, we've been watching you make your way inside.' He giggled. 'We even watched you getting changed into your ridiculous outfit.'

'I hope you enjoyed yourself,' Eden muttered.

'Oh, I did, I did,' Maddox said. 'And we watched you smuggle yourself into the lift and try and use the pass to activate it. I'm guessing that's poor Billy's pass, isn't it?'

Eden said nothing, just kept her eyes fixed on the double doors leading to the boardroom.

'Poor Billy, such an unfortunate accident,' Maddox said, sounding anything but sympathetic. 'I'm surprised you thought Billy even had access down here.'

Eden looked up at Maddox.

He grinned. 'I sent for the lift from down here. It seemed unfair to just leave you in there, wondering what on earth you were going to do.'

They had stopped outside the boardroom where Eden had last seen Max Charon. Maddox opened the doors and urged her inside, a hand on her back. Eden's skin crawled at his touch.

Then she looked across the room and gasped.

'Finn!' she cried out.

Finn was sitting in a chair at the opposite end of the boardroom. It took her a moment to realise that his wrists were tied to the chair with plastic ties. Behind him the great white shark glided past, only the thick glass of the picture window separating the hungry predator from them.

'Eden, what are you doing here?' Finn cried out, struggling against the plastic ties. 'Have they hurt you? Have they — ?'

'No, I'm fine, I'm fine,' Eden said.

Her first instinct was to run over and throw her arms around him, but Maddox grabbed her by the elbow and guided her to another chair, similar to the one Finn was tied to. He pushed her roughly into it. Grabbing her right wrist, he pulled out a black, plastic tie and placed it around her arm.

'No!' Eden shouted and struggled to free herself.

Maddox slapped her across the face.

'Stay still!' he hissed.

'Get your hands off her!' Finn shouted.

Maddox ignored him and snapped the plastic tie around her wrist and the chair leg. He moved to her other side and did the same again. Once she was secured, he quickly patted her down until he found her mobile. He pulled it out of a pocket in her overalls and tossed it on the desk, then perched on the edge.

'I'm guessing that stunt upstairs is something to do with you,' Maddox said.

Eden shrugged. Her cheek stung from the slap, but she wasn't going to let Maddox see that.

'Well, it doesn't matter, Jagger will have sorted them out by now.'

'Eden, what's going on?' Finn said. 'Please, don't tell me you came here to rescue me!'

Eden looked across the room at Finn. There seemed to be such a huge gulf separating them.

'Of course I did,' she said.

She was close to tears, scared and tired, but also full of love for Finn. Her heart had swelled at the sight of him.

Maddox chuckled. 'Oh my life, and they say love is dead. They should, ah, come down here and have a look at you two.'

Finn looked as if he was about to respond, but the door opened and his Uncle Max stepped in, followed by Jagger. Finn's mouth snapped shut.

Maddox leapt off Charon's desk as if he had been electrocuted. Charon ignored him, instead walking over to stand in front of Eden.

'You really are rather a remarkable young woman,' he said, gazing down at her. 'I could use someone like you in the business.'

'That won't happen,' Eden said.

'No, I didn't expect so,' Charon replied. 'Such a shame.'

'Hey, Uncle Max, please don't hurt Eden,' Finn said. 'She has nothing to do with this — please just let her go.'

'Shut your mouth, cuz,' Jagger sneered, jabbing a pointed finger at Finn. 'You've got no say in this, you lost that right when you refused Dad's offer to be part of the business.'

Finn struggled against his restraints for a moment and then stopped and glared at Jagger.

'What are we going to do with you all?' Max Charon said. 'I have to say, Finn, that you and your friends are making life very difficult for me.'

'There's an easy way to solve this,' Finn said. 'Let us go.'

'Don't be such an idiot,' Jagger said, smiling lazily. 'You know that's never going to happen.'

Eden's chest contracted with fear. What did he mean by that? Surely Charon wouldn't resort to murder? Would he?

A sudden, low rumble from upstairs distracted everyone, and Eden felt a shiver travel from the floor through the soles of her feet and up her legs. All faces turned to look at the ceiling.

'What was that?' Maddox said.

'That storm's getting pretty fierce,' Jagger replied. 'Go upstairs and take a look around, see if anything's been damaged.'

Maddox left.

'I think we're going to have to delay the delivery until tomorrow, Dad,' Jagger said.

Charon shook his head thoughtfully. 'We can't, we have to keep packing the crates onto the truck.'

'What are you talking about?' Finn said.

Charon smiled his shark's grin. 'Our next order — a shipment of guns to a London-based outfit. And next month a second delivery to Edinburgh. The career criminal is alive and well and flourishing in modern day Britain. We've got profitable times ahead, my boy. We're going to be rich. Are you sure I can't change your mind about joining us?'

'Yeah, I'm sure,' Finn said.

Eden noticed a flash of movement on the other side of the huge picture window. The shark seemed agitated. Its usual slow cruise was gone, and instead the huge fish was darting in different directions, snapping its jaws at any other fish it passed. It had to be the storm, making it nervous.

'A shame,' Charon said. He turned to Jagger. 'You're right, I'm growing soft in my old age. I've been wasting time.'

'When do you want me to do it?' Jagger said.

'Do it now,' Max Charon replied. 'Kill them both.'

'Wait!' Finn said. 'Uncle Max, you can't be serious!'

Eden pulled against her restraints as panic blossomed in her chest. The hard plastic ties bit into her wrists, too strong to be pulled apart.

'With pleasure,' Jagger said, smiling.

★ ★ ★

From his hiding place, Larry peered through his binoculars and watched the forklift trucks down below, laden with crates, swaying in the howling wind. Larry was sheltered somewhat beneath a rocky outcrop, but even there he could feel how violent the wind was. With his hood up he was protected from much of the rain, but whenever raindrops were driven into his face by the gale force wind, they stung as they smacked against his skin.

Larry couldn't believe they were still working down there. The storm had already caused one accident, forcing a forklift truck off its path and into another one. The crates had come tumbling off and smashed onto the ground, spilling their contents of plastic weaponry all over the yard.

But still they carried on working.

Larry wasn't too concerned about what was going on at Charon Recycling, though. He was more worried about Nina. Both Larry and Nina had agreed that if she felt the sea was too rough to make a return journey from Cinders Hole by dinghy on her own, then she should climb the Chimney after Eden.

He had been sat here in his spot for a while now, his binoculars trained on the hole in the ground where he had seen Eden emerge. The iron grill still lay on the grass beside the hole, but there was no sign of Nina.

Larry decided he'd waited long enough. He had to get down there and find out if Nina was all right, or if she was in trouble. Sneaking around wasn't an option any longer and the workmen down there looked as though they had too much trouble on their hands to notice Larry.

He pulled himself from his shelter in the rocks. The wind immediately smashed into him, knocking him down on the wet grass. Larry scrambled to his feet and the gale force wind slammed into him again, knocking the breath from his lungs.

*This is ridiculous*, he thought. *What do we think we're doing? We should all be inside the youth hostel, drinking and eating while we watch the storm from the comfort of a warm snug.*

This time he managed to stay on his feet and began making his way carefully down the slope. Several times he slipped, or was pushed to the ground by a powerful gust, but finally he made it to the bottom, on the other side of the fence separating him from Charon Recycling. He pushed his fingers through the chain-link fence and looked at the hole in the ground, the opening of the Chimney over Cinders Hole.

'Nina!' he shouted.

There was no point; his voice was snatched away by the wind, and the pounding of the rain made it impossible for anyone to hear him anyway.

He had to get over the fence.

Climbing the fence wasn't going to be a big deal; the problem was getting over there without being seen by the security cameras. But then, surely he would have been noticed by now anyway? No security guards had come dashing out of the building, ready to arrest him. And from the looks of things in the loading facility, they had enough problems with keeping the storm from destroying everything.

Larry decided to risk it.

He scrambled up the fence, over the top and then hung at arm's length to shorten the drop to the ground, before finally letting go. Landing on the soft, wet ground, he slipped and fell. He lay flat for a moment, the rain pounding into him.

Larry clambered to his hands and knees and crawled over to the hole in the ground. Pulling a torch from his jacket, he shone it down into the rocky tunnel.

'Turn that light off, will you!' Nina yelled.

'Sorry!' Larry shouted back.

He angled the torch away slightly so that the beam wasn't shining directly into Nina's eyes, but was close enough to see her. Nina was jammed in the chimney, one arm stretched out above her head and clinging onto a rocky ledge. Her hair was plastered to her skull, and rainwater ran down her face. She didn't look at all happy.

'Are you all right?' Larry shouted, struggling to make himself heard above the howling wind.

'Oh yes, I'm having a great time!' she shouted back. 'We should do this again tomorrow!'

'Seriously?' Larry yelled.

'Of course not! I'm stuck!'

'Hang on, I'll come down to you,' Larry yelled.

Nina looked up at him, eyes wide.

'No, stay where you are, I don't want you slipping and landing on top of me. I can do this, I just need a minute.'

'All right, just take your time,' Larry shouted.

He looked up at the sound of waves crashing against the rocks below them, and another sound, in the distance. Something like a low rumble, something powerful and frightening.

But what could it be?

In the distance he saw it. A massive swell gathering, larger than any he had ever seen. This was going to be a huge wave, a massive wall of torrential water. If they were still here when it hit the rocks, they would be picked up like dolls and thrown out to sea or bashed against the cliff.

'Nina!' Larry yelled, looking back down the Chimney. 'You know what I just said about taking your time?'

Nina craned her head back, squinting.

'Yeah, what about it?'

'Scrub that, you need to get out right now!'

★ ★ ★

Jagger pointed the gun at Finn. Eden couldn't believe what she was seeing. The gun was tiny and made of bright yellow plastic, but she had no doubt it was lethal.

Jagger had a big, nasty grin on his face as he stared at Finn. He didn't seem to be in a rush.

'What are you waiting for?' Max Charon said. 'This is what you wanted all along. Kill him — kill them both.'

'I'm just enjoying the moment,' Jagger said. 'This is fun.'

'Just get on with it,' Charon said. 'We've got more important things to worry about.'

'Jagger — wait, think about what you're doing,' Finn said, straining against his restraints. 'You do this, you're a murderer.'

Jagger tilted his head back and laughed.

'Are you serious, cuz? I'm already a murderer! This is nothing new to me.'

Eden fought to control her breathing. She rotated her wrists inside the plastic ties, their sharp edges biting into her skin. If she made her hands as small as possible, squeezing the fingers and thumb together, she might just be able to pull herself free.

Slowly, doing her best to remain unnoticed, Eden pulled at the plastic ties. Straining against them with every last reserve of strength and determination she had, Eden clenched her jaw at the pain of the plastic biting into the flesh around her wrists. It felt as if she was tearing her skin off in strips.

No good. Maddox had pulled them too tight.

Despair filled Eden's chest. Was this it, then?

Yes. They were going to die down here.

'I'm going upstairs, find out what's going on,' Charon said. 'Come on up when you've finished having your fun.'

'Will do, Da — '

The deep rumble cut him off. The floor, the walls, everything seemed to shiver as the rumble grew louder. Eden kept expecting it to subside, to fade away, but it was growing stronger, louder.

'What's going on now?' Charon said, looking up at the ceiling.

Eden could hear shouting from up above, the clatter of things falling over.

The rumble was finally subsiding. But now a loud snapping sound pulled their attention away from whatever was going on up at ground level.

Eden realised she wasn't going to die at the hands of Jagger Charon after all.

But she was going to die.

A long crack had appeared in the window of Max Charon's glorified aquarium. It had spread outward in zigzags, like a bolt of lightning. With another loud snap it extended even further.

'Please, let us go,' Eden said. 'Untie us, quickly, before the glass shatters.'

Max Charon was already heading for the boardroom doors.

'Leave them!' he shouted at Jagger. 'They are going to die anyway down here.'

Jagger grinned and gave Eden and Finn a little wave. He followed his father out of the boardroom.

'Can you pull yourself free at all?' Finn said.

Eden shook her head. 'I've been trying, but the ties are too tight.'

Finn looked at the huge crack running across the window, a fine tracery of spider's web lines radiating outward. Behind the now almost opaque glass, the shark continued its frantic swimming.

Finn turned back to Eden.

'I love you,' he said.

The window shattered.

Eden just had time to suck in a huge gulp of air before she was knocked over by the powerful rush of water. She landed on her side, her feet kicking out uselessly, her wrists tied to the chair legs as she was dragged across the floor by the powerful current.

Within seconds the room was full of water.

287

Eden couldn't see anything. The water was too churned up. She fought against the restraints with all her strength, but there was no point. The plastic ties were too strong, and the weight of the chair was holding her underwater.

How long could she hold her breath? Eden knew she could hold on for at least two minutes. She had spent plenty of time practising the art of holding her breath. But what was the point? She could do nothing to free herself.

A shape appeared on the edge of her vision, swimming towards her. Was it Finn? Had he freed himself somehow?

Her view was clearing as the water calmed. The blurred shape began to take on more definition.

Eden's chest contracted with cold fear.

This wasn't Finn swimming towards her.

It was the shark.

# 17

The last of the seawater drained past them and down the chimney. Larry had taken the decision to climb down the opening and help Nina. That wave had looked too big and powerful for him to be sitting at the top of the cliff, waiting for that force of nature to smash into him.

Once inside the chimney with Nina he had grabbed her outstretched hand and hauled her up through the tight gap. She had scrambled at the edges, pushing hard against the rocky outcrops with her feet and dragging herself up when her other hand was freed.

Then they had clung to the rock as the world exploded in a maelstrom of rushing water above their heads.

The seawater quickly filled the Chimney and cascaded over them. Larry had squeezed his eyes shut as the force of the water threatened to drag him from his precarious handholds. But he hung on, cheek pressed against the rock.

Finally, the rushing water subsided, and Larry and Nina were left clinging to the sides, coughing and spluttering.

'Let's get out of here,' Larry gasped. 'There might be another wave on its way.'

Nina didn't answer, simply started climbing.

Soon they were both kneeling in the sodden grass, the rain still hammering at them. Nina looked out across the dark, rain-filled ocean. Its surface looked as if it was boiling, but there was no sign of another huge wave heading their way.

'I think we're OK for the moment,' she gasped. 'But we should get inside.'

'I think you're right,' Larry said.

He clambered to his feet, helping Nina up. They staggered past the building, towards the front. Seaweed hung from the chain-link fence, and more clumps of seaweed and broken shells littered the ground. Larry even saw some fish flopping about, gasping for air.

And there were hundreds of pellets of brightly coloured plastic littering the ground, as though the sea had grown angry at this pollution and tried throwing it back.

Hanging on to each other, Nina and Larry started running.

The yard at the front of Charon Recycling looked as if a hurricane had swept through it. Three forklift trucks lay on their sides. Many of the crates had been smashed open, spilling the multi-coloured contents over the yard. The workers were slowly gathering themselves up, getting to their feet.

'Come on, let's get inside,' Nina said. 'We need to find the others.'

\* \* \*

Slowly the shark approached Eden, gliding gracefully through the water. It was so close she could see its eyes were black, like a doll's eyes. And its mouth was lined with pointed, serrated teeth, all overlapping. One chomp with those powerful jaws and the shark could bite her in half.

Eden tensed every muscle in her body, willing herself to remain completely still. Tied to the chair, there was nothing more she could do. Her brain was screaming at her to flee, and every muscle seemed to be twitching with the desire to obey her brain. But she knew that no matter how much she might kick and thrash about, she wasn't going anywhere. All she would do was attract the shark's attention.

Gliding closer, the shark turned at the last moment and swam past her. So graceful as it glided by, the great white was terrifyingly beautiful. Its tail fin kicked out at Eden as the shark propelled itself on its way and smacked her in the side.

She tumbled across the floor, struggling to keep from gasping in pain and letting go of all that precious air in her lungs. When she finally rolled to a stop, she realised her left arm was free.

When she had been batted across the floor by the shark's tail fin, the force of the blow had splintered one of the chair's legs. With much more freedom of movement available, Eden was able to slide her other wrist free.

With a powerful shove of her feet, she swam up, looking for the water's surface. She had to hope that the boardroom hadn't completely filled with seawater yet.

She broke free, gasping for air, sucking it in greedily. There wasn't much room between the surface and the ceiling, but she was able to hold her head comfortably out of the water and take in a few deep breaths.

She took a quick look around. There was nobody else here, at the water's surface. Had Jagger and Max been killed in the sudden, torrential wave of seawater, or had they made it to the lift and managed to make their escape?

Amazingly, the lights in the ceiling were still on, but she expected they would die soon, their electric supply short-circuited by the rising water. And when they did, she would be trapped here in the dark with an angry great white shark prowling.

She had to get out.

But first she had to rescue Finn. Which meant she had to get back down underwater and find him. She couldn't let him die down there.

Taking a deep breath, Eden rolled over and kicked off against the ceiling, pushing herself underwater once more. The current had settled down and Eden was able to see better. A fish darted by, blue and yellow striped, and she saw a large crab scuttling across the carpeted floor.

Eden swam over the massive board-room table. The chairs had been scattered.

She spotted Finn. He was lying on his side, still strapped to the chair. Eden swam towards him, looking for any sign of movement, hoping he was still alive. As she approached him he lifted his head, his hair billowing in the water, and stared at her with bulging eyes. He couldn't hold his breath for much longer, that was obvious, but even so he was flicking his head at her, trying to tell her to go away and save herself.

Eden took a look at the plastic ties, holding him to the chair. Despair washed over her as she saw what Jagger had done. She had been hoping she could slide Finn's arms and the plastic ties down the chair legs and over the ends to set him free. But Jagger had fastened Finn's wrists above a cross bar. There was no way of getting the ties off. Not without a knife or a pair of scissors.

The shark passed them, gliding slowly by. It didn't have much room down here and Eden was scared it might panic and begin thrashing and snapping those jaws at anything nearby. Like Finn and Eden.

Seeing the shark reminded her of the

paper shark Max Charon had made and given to her that first time she had met him. And her chest exploded with hope as she pictured Charon using the scissors to make the finishing touches to his origami shark.

The scissors! He had put them in a drawer in his desk when he had finished with them.

If they were still there . . .

Eden turned, flicking her head from side to side, looking for the desk, strands of her hair floating around her face as if they were alive. She spotted the desk and swam over to it. It had been dragged across the room by the strength of the water rushing in, but it was still upright. Eden pulled open the drawer — and there were the scissors, as she had hoped.

Her heart thumping, she snatched up the scissors and swam back to Finn. Grabbing his right hand, she snipped the plastic tie apart and his wrist was free. Once she had cut the other plastic tie, Finn kicked off the floor and shot up to the surface.

Eden followed him.

In the now tiny gap between the sea-water and the ceiling, Finn was coughing and spluttering and sucking in air.

The tiny sliver of air was narrowing as the water was still rising. Eden and Finn had to tilt their heads back to keep their mouths free of seawater.

And there was still a great white, man-eating shark circling below them.

'We've got to get to the stairs!' Eden gasped.

Finn nodded.

They both took a deep breath and disappeared beneath the water's surface once more.

Eden spotted the doors, pushed wide open by the flood of water. The shark swam in front of them, its tail fin kicking faster than before, propelling it through the water like a perfect swimming machine.

*It's getting agitated*, Eden thought. *We need to get out of here before it decides to take a bite out of us.*

Once the shark had swum by, she

and Finn kicked themselves towards the doorway. Just outside was the stairway — and at the top of that was fresh air and freedom.

Eden was in front. With a few powerful kicks of her feet and strokes with her arms, she was into the stairwell. The stairs switched back on themselves, and this lower section was still under water. With Finn beside her, she swam up and around the stairway, and suddenly her head was above water.

Finn surfaced beside her, coughing and spluttering. He wiped his hair off his face.

'I thought we were dead!' he gasped.

'You weren't the only one!' Eden said, taking deep breaths of the precious, sweet air.

They helped each other out of the water and sat on the steps. Eden pictured the great white shark, swimming around and around, trapped. And up above them she could hear the wind and the rain battering the recycling facility.

Finn lay on his back against the stairs

and started laughing.

'What are you laughing at?' Eden said.

'I'm laughing because I'm alive!' he gasped.

Eden started laughing too and lay down beside him. Finn took her hand.

'We need to get out of here.'

'I know, I just need a second or two,' Eden said, panting.

Finn pulled her close. 'You're amazing, you know that?'

Eden nodded and smiled. 'Of course I am.'

Their lips met. Eden tasted seawater as they kissed.

'Aww, how sweet.'

They pulled apart and looked up. Jagger Charon was standing on the steps above them.

And he was holding a shotgun.

Just like Eden and Finn, he was dripping wet but he was alive. Eden briefly wondered if Max Charon had escaped too. He must have done — he had been in front of Jagger when they were making their escape. He had to be up there somewhere.

'Jagger,' Finn said, clambering to his feet, 'put the gun down, let us go. It's over.'

Jagger smiled that shark's grin again and levelled the gun at Finn.

'You always were annoying, little cousin,' he said.

He squeezed the trigger.

The deafening shotgun blast echoed around the stairwell as Finn smacked into Eden and pulled her into the water. Still holding onto her, Finn kicked out and propelled them deeper into the turbulent water as she heard the muffled sound of the gun being fired again. The shotgun pellets stung Eden's back and legs, but they had lost a lot of their power as soon as they hit the water.

Tumbling and twirling, she reached out for Finn.

And saw tendrils of red blood curling through the water like smoke.

Finn! He'd been shot.

Eden grabbed him by his shirt, pulling at him, dragging him closer. He turned, grabbed at Eden and held on.

He'd been shot in the shoulder, Eden could see the scarlet blood floating away from the wound.

They were back at the bottom of the stairs, with no way out except back to where Jagger was standing guard with the shotgun. Finn, his long hair swirling around his head, pointed to the board-room. He was right, they could swim back to the pocket of air under the ceiling — but how long before they ran out of oxygen?

And besides, there was the shark. The scent of blood in the water would drive it into a frenzy, and Eden and Finn would have no chance. It would home in on them like a missile.

As though she had conjured the monster up simply by thinking about it, the great white suddenly appeared. It was headed straight for them, its mouth opening in anticipation.

There was no time to worry about Jagger waiting for them with his shotgun; if they didn't move now they were shark food. Eden and Finn kicked out, propelling themselves up the stairs, around the switchback in the stairwell and back to the surface.

As they pulled themselves from the water, the very first thing Eden saw were Jagger's boots. He had come down the steps until he had reached the waterline, waiting to see if Eden and Finn would come back.

She looked up. Jagger raised his arms, holding the shotgun high and ready to smash it stock first on their heads. A look of pure hatred contorted his face, pulling his lips back in an ugly snarl.

Eden grabbed an ankle and yanked, hard.

Jagger flipped over on his back, hitting the steps with a crack and yelling in pain. With Finn's help, Eden dragged Jagger under the water.

'Hey, guys!' Larry shouted from the top of the steps.

He ran down to them, grabbed Finn by his uninjured arm and hauled him up out of the water. Eden followed them.

Until she was pulled up short by a hand grabbing her ankle and pulling her down.

She smacked against the steps face first, grunting at the shock. Before she had a chance to recover, Jagger was dragging her into the water.

Eden twisted and kicked out, but her foot connected with thin air. Suddenly Jagger was on top of her, his fingers raking down her shirt as he tried to get a grip, tried to pull her deeper into the water.

Eden lashed out, kicking and punching. The momentum overbalanced them, and both Eden and Jagger fell into the water with a splash. Still fighting, they sank deeper. No matter how hard Eden thrashed or punched and kicked, Jagger refused to let go of her. He was bigger than her. Stronger.

But he couldn't stay underwater for long. And Eden was sure she could hold her breath longer than he could. Except, now they had reached the bottom of the stairs and Jagger was on top of her, pinning her to the floor.

Eden struggled against his weight, but it was no use, she was trapped.

Her eyes widened as she saw Jagger raising his fist above his head.

Jagger punched Eden in the stomach, and her precious air exploded from her lungs as she gasped in pain. With all her years of practice and training in the water, instinct kicked in and Eden managed to keep from trying to breathe in. If she had, her lungs would have filled with water and her body would have gone into meltdown as it tried to expel all that fluid.

But she had no air left, and Jagger was raising his fist to punch her again.

Eden shook her head desperately, tried to pull herself free, but his weight had her pinned down.

Jagger was smiling as his fist descended, leaving trails of fine water bubbles behind it.

This last punch would finish Eden off.

A flurry of movement, a grey, blurred shape and a brief flash of teeth, and

Jagger was snatched off Eden as though a rope had been tied around his waist and then some invisible force had yanked hard, dragging him away.

Not pausing to see what had happened, Eden swam for the stairwell. Just as she began to head for the surface, she twisted her head for one quick look to see if Jagger was after her again.

Eden caught a brief glimpse of the shark swimming away, but the rapidly growing cloud of red obscured her view.

Eden swam up the stairs and surfaced, gasping. Larry was there, hand outstretched.

'Oh man, I am so glad to see you! I was just about to dive in there and go looking for you.'

Eden took his hand.

'Just get me out of here, will you?' she gasped.

'Where's Jagger?' Larry said.

Eden just shook her head and sat on the steps, water dripping from her hair and her face.

Once she had got her breath back,

305

Larry helped her up the steps.

'Where's Finn, is he OK?' Eden demanded.

'Don't worry, he's fine, he's with Nina — and Doug and Ellie,' Larry replied. 'We just need to get him to a hospital, get that shoulder seen to. I have a feeling it might be broken.'

Eden shivered and lowered her head. She was growing cold, and she couldn't rid herself of the sight of that shark disappearing in a cloud of scarlet as it swam away with Jagger.

Larry wrapped an arm around her shoulders.

'We need to get you warm and dry.'

'I just want to see Finn,' Eden said.

Larry stopped walking. 'Oh no.'

Eden looked up.

Doug, Ellie, Nina and Finn were huddled together in a group. Finn was clutching his injured arm, and he looked pale and unsteady.

Max Charon had a gun trained on them. He glanced over at Eden.

'Where's Jagger? Where's my boy?'

'Jagger's dead,' she said. 'He's shark food.'

The old man's face turned pale.

'No, I don't believe you.' He stood there, holding the gun on Finn and the others, while he absorbed what he had just been told. And then his face slowly hardened.

'You killed him. And now, I'm going to kill you, all of you.'

He lifted the gun.

'Put the weapon down!'

Charon slowly lowered the shotgun as police streamed through the doors and into the lobby. Within seconds, Charon's gun had been taken from him and he was being cuffed and led away. Eden saw Tom Maddox was sitting in the back of one of the police cars already, parked just outside the doors.

'I didn't realise you'd called the police,' Eden said to Doug.

'I didn't,' Doug replied, looking as mystified as Eden felt.

'I think it was him,' Ellie said, pointing.

Jim was running across the lobby towards Eden. He wrapped his arms around her and held her tight.

'Are you all right?' he said, pulling back so that he could get a good look at her.

'I'm fine, Eden said, laughing with relief. 'How did you even know we were here?'

Jim pointed at Larry. 'He told me what you were all planning. I thought it over for a while and then when I'd come to the conclusion you were all insane, I called the police. And I'm glad I did, and I'm glad they took me seriously.'

'So am I,' Eden said.

Gently she disentangled herself from Jim's arms and walked over to Finn. Taking care not to hurt his injured shoulder, she wrapped her arms around him.

*I love you*, he'd said to her just before the window shattered.

'Hey,' she said quietly, looking into those beautiful eyes of his. 'I love you too.'

# 18

Nerves and excitement fluttered through Eden's stomach. What did she even think she was doing? She wasn't ready for this, she wasn't even sure she ever would be ready for this, and yet here she was.

Closing her eyes, Eden took a deep breath.

*Come on, calm yourself down. You can do this.*

The swell of the ocean lifted her, then gently let her down again. The movement was familiar, comforting. Eden opened her eyes, looked over her shoulder. She had to stay alert now; the time for nerves was over with.

Somehow — she had no idea how — Eden had made it into the finals of the surfing championships. Not just in her class, but the actual finals. And everything now counted on this final surf.

The perfect wave was building. Eden began paddling.

*Come on,* she thought. *You do this every day. This is the thing you love, riding waves on a surfboard. Just because today you happen to be in the finals of the championships, doesn't mean it's any different.*

Eden glanced at the beach ahead, at the crowds watching, at the viewing tower where the judges were observing her through their binoculars, and the photographers from the surfing magazines.

*Yeah, right.*

The surfboard Jim had made for Eden had served her well. There had been times when she almost believed it had a mind of its own, that it was doing more of the work of riding the waves than she was. Despite her lack of practice and familiarisation with her new board, Eden had worked her way steadily through the competition to get to this day.

She glanced ahead again at the beach as she continued paddling. Eden knew

Finn was there with the others. He had not been able to surf because of his fractured shoulder. But he had been out there every day, his arm in a sling, watching Eden do her thing out on the waves and cheering her on.

It was strange to think that only two weeks ago she had believed him to be working for Max and Jagger, spying on Eden and her friends. She had apologised so much that Finn had eventually banned her from saying sorry any more.

She did tease him, though, that she hadn't actually seen him surfing yet, and did he even know how? And how come Jim had been unable to find any evidence of him entering surfing competitions, or being affiliated with any surfing organisations?

Finn had to remind her that he'd never used his own name in the surfing community, because of the bad press attached to it.

Eden had felt a little stupid over that and kicked herself. But when Jim said he hadn't been able to find Finn on the online surfing registers, she had been so upset she hadn't stopped to think about what name he was searching for.

She had simply believed everything Maddox had been telling her.

At least that was all over with now, and with Max Charon behind bars and his entire seedy operation exposed, Simeon was no longer facing a prosecution for trespassing and causing damage. Something he hadn't done in the first place. The entire thing had been an accident at the recycling facility, and Jagger had taken the opportunity to get his revenge on Simeon by framing him for it.

Even the nightmares about the shark, its jaws closing around Jagger Charon, had begun to recede. The great white had attacked out of instinct, of course, but Eden was still grateful to it — even if she'd had to force herself to go back in the water.

The shark, along with the other marine life that Max Charon had illegally collected, had been set free.

But not before a tracker had been attached to the great white, so that it could be monitored.

Thankfully the powerful predator had quickly left the local area and headed out to the deeper ocean, leaving the Cornish waters safe for swimming and surfing in.

Pushing all these thoughts away and clearing her mind, Eden pushed herself up on to her knees. There was no need to look back at the wave, she could feel its power starting to lift her. The nerves had all gone now. For the next few moments she would forget all about the competition, about winning or losing.

As she jumped to her feet, positioning herself to ride the wave, Eden was lost in the moment. In the power of the ocean.

The crest of the wave was behind and above her. Eden's surfboard was gliding over the water as she surfed at an angle towards the beach. The wave arched over her, and she was in the tube.

She was in heaven.

'You were amazing!' Finn said, wrapping his good arm around Eden and squeezing her tight.

'I know, I know!' Eden said, laughing. 'But was I amazing enough?'

Finn answered by planting a kiss on her lips.

'Of course you were,' he said, pulling back. 'You've got this, you're going to be the champion.'

Doug clapped her on the back.

'Yeah, too right. And when we get back to the youth hostel tonight, we should have a party to celebrate!'

'You and your parties,' Nina said, smiling at Eden and giving her a wink. 'But for once, I'm in agreement. We should definitely celebrate.'

Eden laughed and said, 'Don't you think you're all counting your chickens before they're hatched? What if I don't win?'

'We'll celebrate anyway,' Ellie said.

Larry placed a hand on Eden's

shoulder and smiled. 'Absolutely.'

'You did good, real good,' Jim said, giving Eden a hug. 'Watching you out there, I knew I'd been right in thinking I was making that surfboard for you. It's like the two of you become one, when you're out on the waves.'

'Hey, listen, they're about to make the announcements!' Finn said excitedly, squeezing Eden's hand.

Eden looked out at the sea, at the waves twinkling in the sun and rolling in to the beach. And then she turned and gazed at Finn, at his face upturned and looking at the judges. Waiting, expectant, hopeful.

And Eden decided then and there that it truly didn't matter whether she won this surfing championship or not.

With Finn in her life she already was a winner.

We do hope that you have enjoyed reading this large print book.

Did you know that all of our titles are available for purchase?

We publish a wide range of high quality large print books including:
**Romances, Mysteries, Classics
General Fiction
Non Fiction and Westerns**

Special interest titles available in large print are:
**The Little Oxford Dictionary
Music Book, Song Book
Hymn Book, Service Book**

Also available from us courtesy of Oxford University Press:
**Young Readers' Dictionary
(large print edition)
Young Readers' Thesaurus
(large print edition)**

For further information or a free brochure, please contact us at:
**Ulverscroft Large Print Books Ltd.,
The Green, Bradgate Road, Anstey,
Leicester, LE7 7FU, England.
Tel:** (00 44) 0116 236 4325
**Fax:** (00 44) 0116 234 0205

# TWICE IN A LIFETIME

## Jo Bartlett

It's been eighteen months since Anna's husband Finn died. Craving space to consider her next steps, she departs the city for the Cornish coast and the isolated Myrtle Cottage. But the best-laid plans often go awry, and when Anna's beloved dog Albie leads her away from solitude and into the path of Elliott, the owner of the nearby adventure centre, their lives become intertwined. As Anna's attraction to Elliott grows, so does her guilt at betraying Finn, until she remembers his favourite piece of advice: you only live once . . .

# WILD SPIRIT

## Dawn Knox

It's Rae's dream to sail away across oceans on her family's boat, the *Wild Spirit* — but in 1939 the world is once again plunged into conflict, and her travel plans must be postponed. When Hitler's forces trap the Allies on the beaches of Dunkirk, Rae sails with a fleet of volunteer ships to attempt the impossible and rescue the desperate servicemen. However, her bravery places more lives than her own in jeopardy — including that of Jamie MacKenzie, the man she's known and loved for years . . .

# RETURN TO TASMANIA

## Alan C. Williams

Heading back from Sydney to her idyllic childhood home in Tasmania, Sandie's priorities are to recover from a bullet wound, reconsider her future in the police, and spend time with her sister and niece. But even as the plane lands, she senses that a fellow passenger is not all he seems. When a series of suspicious events follow her arrival, the mystery man reveals himself as Adam, who has been sent to protect Sandie's family as they become embroiled in the fall-out following the double-crossing of a dangerous criminal.

# THE ENGLISH AU PAIR

## Chrissie Loveday

Stella Lazenby flies to Spain to work as an au pair for Isabel and Ignacio Mendoza, looking after their sons Juan and Javier. The parents are charming, the boys delightful — and then there's the handsome Stefano, who becomes more than a friend . . . But all is not as perfect as it seems. Housekeeper Maria resents Stella's presence, and Isabel worries that her husband is hiding secrets. Then Stefano is accused of stealing from Ignacio's company, and Stella doesn't know what to believe . . .

# DANGER FOR DAISY

## Francesca Capaldi

Mature student Daisy Morgan plucks up her courage to attend a get-together — only to cannon straight into a handsome gentleman, spilling her drink all over his smart suit into the bargain! To make matters worse, he turns out to be Seth, her flatmates' archaeologist friend. After this unconventional meeting, sparks quickly kindle between the pair, and Daisy accompanies Seth to a dig on a remote island. But danger lurks on Sealfarne — and they are about to unearth it . . .

# THE BRIDE IS MISSING

## Anne Hewland

Cat is meant to be marrying Stephen after a whirlwind romance. So why is she now waking up on a small Welsh island, still in her hen party outfit? She initially thinks it's a pre-wedding prank — but soon it becomes apparent that the reality is much more sinister. Along with Greg, the man who discovered her when she woke by the beach, Cat is drawn into the web of intrigue which has entangled both her fiancé and her best friend . . .